This novel is ent
The names, characters and incidents in it are the work of the author's imagination. Any resemblance or act relating to any persons, living or dead, locations or events involving them, is entirely alleged or coincidental.

Published by BSA Publishing 2021 who assert the right that no part of this publication may be reproduced, stored in a retrieval system or transmitted by any means without the prior permission of the publishers.

Copyright @ B.L.Faulkner 2019 who

Asserts the moral right to be identified as

the author of this work

ISBN 978-1-9161633-0-0

Proof read/editing by Zeldos

BOOKS IN THE DCS PALMER SERIES (SO FAR)

BOOK 1 FUTURE RICHES
BOOK 2 FELT TIP MURDERS
BOOK 3 A KILLER IS CALLING
BOOK 4 POETIC JUSTICE
BOOK 5 LOOT
BOOK 6 I'M WITH THE BAND
BOOK 7 BURNING AMBITION
BOOK 8 TAKEAWAY TERROR
BOOK 9 MINISTRY OF MURDER
BOOK 10 THE BODY BUILDER
BOOK 11 SUCCESSION
BOOK 12 THE BLACK ROSE
BOOK 13 LAPTOPS CAN KILL

BEN NEVIS & THE GOLD DIGGER SERIES

BOOK 1 TURKISH DELIGHT
BOOK 2 NATIONAL TREASURE

FACTUAL BOOKS

LONDON CRIME

An in-depth history of the gangs, geezers and heists in the UK from 1930s until present day includes Brinks Mat, Krays, Richardsons, Great Train Robbery, Hatton Garden, John Palmer etc etc.

UK SERIAL KILLERS

44 Serial Killers from the 1930s to the present day, their lives, crimes and punishments. 44 serial killers including Brady, Neilsen, Bellfield, West, Sutcliffe, Shipman and Christie in chronological order detailing their lives, their killings, and their punishments. Not for the faint hearted!

****

NOTE.   All Barry Faulkner's books are in 14point easy-read typeface.

THE PALMER CASES BACKGROUND

Justin Palmer started off on the beat as a London policeman in the late 1970s and is now Detective Chief Superintendent Palmer running the Metropolitan Police Force's Serial Murder Squad from New Scotland Yard.

Not one to pull punches, or give a hoot for political correctness if it hinders his inquiries, Palmer has gone as far as he will go in the Met and he knows it. Master of the one-line put-down and a slave to his sciatica, he can be as nasty or as nice as he likes.

The early 2000s was a time of re-awakening for Palmer as the Information Technology revolution turned forensic science, communication and information gathering skills upside down. Realising the value of this revolution to crime solving, Palmer co-opted Detective Sergeant Gheeta Singh into his team. DS Singh has a degree in IT and was given the go ahead to update Palmer's department with all the computer hard and software she wanted, most of which she wrote herself and some of which are, shall we say, of a grey area when it comes to privacy laws, data protection and accessing certain restricted databases.

Together with their small team of favourite officers that Palmer co-opts from other departments as needed, and one civilian computer clerk called Claire they take on the serial killers of the UK.

On the personal front Palmer has been married to his 'princess', or Mrs P. as she is known to everybody, for nearly thirty years. The romance blossomed after the young Detective Constable Palmer arrested most of her family, who were a bunch of South London petty criminals, in the 1960's. They live in a nice house in the London suburb of Dulwich Village, and have a faithful English springer called Daisy.

Gheeta Singh lives alone in a fourth floor Barbican apartment, her parents having arrived on these shores as a refugee family fleeing from Idi Amin's Uganda. Since then her father and brothers have built up a very successful computer parts supply company, in which it was assumed Gheeta would take an active role on graduating from university. She had other ideas on this, as well as the arranged marriage that her mother and aunts still try to coerce her into. Gheeta has two loves, police work and

technology, and thanks to Palmer she has her
dream job.

The old copper's nose and gut feelings of
Palmer, combined with the modern IT skills of
DS Singh makes them an unlikely but successful
team. All their cases involve multiple killings,
twisting and turning through red herrings and
hidden clues, and keeping the reader in suspense
until the very end.

****

BURNING AMBITION

CHAPTER 1

On the 13th July 1955 Ruth Ellis was the last person to be sentenced to death and hanged in the UK. If Robin Hartley-Lansdown had had his way, she wouldn't have been the last.

The Honourable Justice Hartley-Lansdown took a deep breath, looked up from his case notes and peered down on the crowded but silent Court Number One at Southwark Crown Court over which he presided. His mood was as foul as the weather outside, where dark clouds hung from the sky threatening to unload their wet content at any moment.

'Take them from here to a place of execution, where they shall be hanged by the neck until dead.' That was what he'd like to say, but of course he could not.

There was an air of apprehension in the courtroom, and Hartley-Lansdown liked that. The theatrics of the British judicial system resonated with him; he liked to be the centre of attention, and he liked the power that was invested in him as a Crown Court Judge. Hartley-Lansdown was one of the elite class of Britain; he knew it, and he loved it. What he mistakenly thought was respect shown towards him by others in the legal profession because of his high position was more often than not just the observance of the ridiculous judicial protocol left over from the feudal middle ages, that had never been updated to reflect the modern world: the robes and insignia, the wig, the standing and the bowing when he entered the court, and the required deference that was expected of the ushers and the defence and prosecuting lawyers. Hartley-Lansdown, and every other judge in the United Kingdom, was perfectly capable of doing the job in a suit and tie, or even jeans and a tee-shirt, but the elite had to maintain their power base in society somehow; in Hartley-Lansdown's case it had been through inherited family wealth, private education, Eton, Cambridge, and a fast-track legal career through his father's Law Chambers at Lincoln's Inn. Hartley-Lansdown had not only been born with a silver spoon in his mouth, he had a whole drawer of them in there.

Privately he despised the criminal element that was presented before him daily for judgement and sentencing. He realised that ninety percent of them would have his beloved Bentley coupe into a dodgy breaker's yard at the slightest opportunity, file the indentifying numbers off and then ship it out to the Middle

East in a container within a week if they could get their thieving hands on it. The age-old social boundaries of *'them and us'* still existed for Hartley-Lansdown and his circle of friends, and he had no intention of letting that boundary be broken on his watch.

It was a trio of *'them'* that stood in the dock before him now. All three had been found guilty by a jury of their peers of a rather vicious assault on staff at a suburban London Post Office as the security company delivered money to top up the ATM machine. A good flogging and many years of hard labour breaking rocks on a desolate moor would have been Hartley-Lansdown's preferred sentence if he were able to give it, but he wasn't. He looked at the three defendants, feeling a surge of mental power in his body. He nodded to the Clerk of the Court, who returned it, and then addressed the defendants.

'The accused shall rise before the Judge.'

The three of them stood, as did the three security officers they were handcuffed to. Hartley-Lansdown cleared his throat.

'The three of you have been found guilty of a most vicious and prolonged physical attack on people going about their normal daily business; an attack that has resulted in severe trauma and mental anxiety being forced upon them, probably for a considerable number of years, if not their entire lives. None of you has shown any remorse for this act, and your criminal records show all of you have committed past crimes of a similar nature in the pursuit of financial gain. I have read both the medical and psychiatric reports that your defence counsel asked to be produced, no doubt in a vain hope that one or the other might show a flaw in your mental state on which to hang the blame for your actions; but both reports state that you are all in full control of your actions, and fully aware of what the consequences on other people could be.'

He paused for a moment and then shifted his gaze from one to the other as he read out the sentences.

'Peter Shore, this Court sentences you to fourteen years in Her Majesty's Prison. Alli Kalhoud, this Court sentences you to fourteen years in Her Majesty's Prison. Robert Kershaw, this Court sentences you to fourteen years in Her Majesty's Prison. In all three sentences, parole will not be granted before a term of ten years has been served. Take them away.'

As the three were escorted out of sight down the dock steps to the waiting prison transport, a few stifled sobs and murmurs could be heard from the public gallery. Relatives of career criminals rarely made a big fuss in court or shouted abuse at the judge; they knew it would make no difference to the sentence and might even put them on a charge if it was too obscene.

The clerk addressed the court once the dock was clear.

'All rise.'

Justice Hartley-Lansdown left by the door behind his throne that led into his dressing chamber, where the clerk and usher helped disrobe him and hang his garments of office in a large Victorian wardrobe, to be brushed and made ready for tomorrow. Another day of justice done, and another three bodies for the Governor of Brixton Prison to squeeze into his already overcrowded cells.

Outside at the rear of the court buildings, Peter Shore, Alli Kalhoud and Robert Kershaw left the building, bowing their heads against the rain that was beginning to fall as they were ushered into their separate barred cubicles inside a waiting prison van. The doors were slammed and bolted, and their relevant sentencing paperwork handed over from the officer of HM Court Security to the officer of HM Prison Security, who climbed into the van's cab as the driver started the engine. They waited as the heavy steel security gates slid open to let them pass into the small security compound, where they waited again until the gates behind them closed with a metallic thud. The roller shutter security door to the outside world in front of them jerked its way upwards, and then they were given the green light to leave the court premises and make their way to Brixton Prison to deposit the prisoners on their first day of fourteen years' detention.

****

CHAPTER 2

The plain squad car, its blues flashing and reflecting off the Thames' rippling surface through the falling darkness of the night, pulled up outside the old disused Victorian dock side warehouse on the quayside in Greenwich.

Detective Chief Superintendent Palmer got out, wincing slightly as his sciatica pricked his right thigh. Bending into the stiff wind, he held his battered trilby firmly in place on his head and stood looking up at the five storeys of dark brickwork towering above him as his second in command, Detective Sergeant Singh, came around from the other side of the car to join him, her iPad at the ready. Palmer smiled to himself as he buttoned up his thick overcoat; he didn't think he could recall a time that DS Singh hadn't had her iPad clutched firmly beside her. It wasn't so long ago that a DS would have had a pencil and notebook! Times changed fast these days.

The call had come on his mobile just as he had returned from taking his dog, Daisy the Springer for her late-night walk through Dulwich, and was about to follow Mrs P. upstairs to bed. The information was scant, but the news that three bodies were involved was enough to click his brain into gear and to ask for a car to pick him up, and for Control to call DS Singh and tell her to be ready to be picked up from her Barbican apartment on his way through; a bit of a lengthy detour, but with the victims already dead there wasn't any great hurry.

'Bit of a wind round here,' he remarked, turning up his collar.

'Comes off the river, guv. Nice in the summer though,' DS Singh replied as they skirted around a fire engine being packed up by its crew getting ready to leave. They walked towards a Judas door in the corner of the huge double metal doors of the warehouse, that once would have seen empty lorries enter and then leave laden with all kinds of imported goods from the far-flung corners of the world.

Once through the Judas door they found themselves inside what was now just a massive shell of a building; all the floors and internal walls were gone. Long thick steel joists kept the exterior walls from caving in and standing upright, the joists themselves supported by huge concrete pillars every five metres. Around the bottom of the walls was the scattered evidence of rough sleepers having used the place for shelter, and the tell-tale pieces of silver paper amongst it showed addicts had also found privacy inside these walls. But that wasn't of any concern to DCS Palmer and his Serial Murder Squad. What was of concern was the blackened shell of a burnt-out prison van in the middle of the concrete floor resting on its wheel rims, the tyres having been cremated. The area around the van was protected by 'crime scene keep out' blue and white striped tape stretched between poles, giving the van a good twenty metre berth all round. A line of white protection suited SOCA officers were doing a knee search of the floor, and 'snappers' – police photographers – were taking pictures of the inside through the open back doors. The smell of burnt rubber hung pungently in the air.

A uniformed inspector alerted to their arrival came over and greeted them with a stern look on his face. He introduced himself.

'Inspector Rayson, Greenwich East Division, sir.'

They shook hands, and Palmer introduced DS Singh.

'What have we got here then, Inspector, I understand that there are three bodies involved?'

'Correct, and all in the back of that van. We assume they are the three prisoners that were being transported inside it – seems like somebody didn't want them to get back to their cells. Not a pretty sight. The bodies are still inside the cages until Forensics are finished, and then the Pathology boys can take them away.'

Palmer winced.

'Christ! That's not a very nice scene to imagine. Do we have any information on who they were?'

'We got the Court inventory sent through with all their personal details.'

Rayson held out a sheaf of papers which DS Singh took.

'Mind you, we can't confirm the bodies are those of the three prisoners listed until we get DNA matches. They're burnt so badly that a visual identification against their mugshots isn't any good.'

He gave Palmer a false smile.

'So over to your team, sir, and good luck. Not a very pleasant crime as you can appreciate.'

Palmer took a deep breath.

'Indeed not. Well, as it's on your turf Inspector my Sergeant will keep you in the loop. I suppose that for a start we can assume that whoever did it knew this warehouse was here and empty, so they could very well be locals and already on your radar.'

'Bit heavy duty for our local faces, sir. We've a couple of armed robbery types, but mostly petty thieves round here; murder is a bit out of their league. Have fun, and call if I can help.'

Rayson gave a salute, nodded to DS Singh and walked away. Palmer gave Singh a questioning look.

'Now I'd have thought that if all he has to fill his days with are petty thieves and an armed robbery once in a blue moon, he'd leap at the chance to get involved in something like this.'

'No, guv.'

'No?'

She shook her head.

'He's not that sort of copper, guv. He likes his desk and the easy life, with the big pension at the end of it. He'll probably end up a Deputy Commissioner or higher.'

'Tut tut, Sergeant, you are beginning to sound a bit like me. I sense a hint of sarcasm.'

An individual completely covered head-to-toe in a white paper protection suit had made his way over to them and was within earshot of the last remark.

'Heaven forbid. One sarcastic old bugger on the force is enough, Sergeant.'

Reg Frome was head of Criminal Forensics and ran the elite Murder Team of SOCA officers. He and Palmer were once both new recruits at the Hendon College in their first months on the force, and had worked together on several cases since as they both moved up the ranks. A rotund, jolly-looking individual, he lowered his face mask and beamed a welcome towards Palmer.

'Justin my old friend, how are you?'

He removed his plastic gloves and they shook hands.

'I'm fine, Reg. What have we got here then?'

Frome ignored him and nodded towards DS Singh.

'Sergeant Singh, always a pleasure to see you, my dear. I see you haven't managed to get away from this irascible old devil yet then?'

Gheeta smiled. She liked Reg Frome; he'd worked with Palmer's team many times in the past, and she thought of him as a rather soft old uncle.

'I'm very well, Mr Frome. This looks like a nasty one, lots of SOCA activity...'

'It *is* a nasty one, Sergeant. Hang on, we'll get you both kitted out and then you can take a look.'

He went off and quickly returned with two pairs of slip-on shoe protectors and two lower face masks.

'Here, put these on and follow me.'

When Palmer and Singh were correctly dressed, Frome lifted the crime scene tape and let them through to follow him round to the back of the van.

'It's a pretty awful mess in there, Justin,' he said, turning to DS Singh. 'Definitely not the kind of thing a young lady wants to see.'

Gheeta smiled at him.

'Very considerate of you Mr Frome, but I've seen a few pretty awful things so I'll probably be okay.'

They moved forward and peered inside. The three barred prisoner cubicles were open, the metal bars scorched black as was the rest of the interior. Inside each cubicle was the burnt body of a prisoner, the charred remains barely distinguishable as human. The flesh had been burnt off the bones, some of which had partly disintegrated in the heat leaving a hardly discernible skeletal shape, with dark flakes of burnt flesh clinging on in places. The skulls were black, the eye and nose sockets empty, and small cracks were visible in the bone where the heat had expanded the brain tissue until the softest part of the skull gave way and let it bubble out. Forensic officers were working carefully through each cubicle, photographing and evidence-bagging any loose material before the bodies could be taken away for their post mortems.

'Christ!'

Palmer was taken aback by the sight. DS Singh fought back the nausea and turned away, gulping in air.

'I did warn you – not very nice, eh? But not as bad as it looks – well, not for those three anyway.'

'How come?' Palmer asked.

'Pathologist had a quick examination and said they'd each been shot in the head before being incinerated. Single shot from the back, execution style; .22 bullets so enough power to penetrate the brain and kill them, but not enough velocity to exit the skull. The bullets will be removed at the post-mortems so with a bit of luck we can match them to the gun if it's a 'rental' and see if it's on our database.'

'A rental?' asked Gheeta,

Frome nodded.

'Yes, it's five years for owning a pistol so most of the gun crime in the UK involves a 'rental' firearm, one that's owned by a gang or individual who rents it out to others for use at a crime, such as armed robbery; then they return it and the cycle repeats. The same gun is often identified as being used in different crimes in different parts of the country; we can identify it by the marks left along the bullets by the hard steel of the barrel against the soft lead of a bullet when fired. If the marks tally, then the gun does too.'

Palmer nodded.

'I'll bet this is a rental. This is a professional execution if ever I saw one, and those boys don't use the same tool twice.'

He walked towards the front of the van.

'Am I going to find the burnt remains of the driver and guard in the cab?'

Frome shook his head.

'The cab's empty, no sign of them.'

'Really? Where are they then?'

'Not in there, that's for sure. No trace of them. Rayson's men did a search round the premises and the neighbourhood, but still no sign of them. You're not going to get much from me on this one, Justin. The fire was obviously set and whoever did it probably used an accelerant to get it going, as there's not much combustible stuff in the back of an all-steel prison van. If they used paraffin or petrol the heat would clean off any prints, which leaves a pretty blank canvas with very little residue for my people to work on. The saving grace is that the fire brigade used CO2 extinguishers to put it out so we might find something, but I'm not hopeful. I've got a sample of the embers so I'll get a gas chromatograph test done in the morning which will tell us the accelerant used.'

'A gas what?' asked Gheeta.

Palmer laughed.

'Are you trying to get a transfer to Forensics, Sergeant?'

'I wish she was,' said Frome. 'I've got officers who use it all the time and have no idea how it works. I'll explain: the gas chromatograph is a simple test to find which chemical has been used to aid combustion in a fire. A sample of the fire debris is taken and put into a container and heated; the gas given off is then passed through the chromatograph and a printout taken in the shape of a graph. The graph shows a series of peaks, with the largest being the culprit accelerant, and the size of that peak determining the actual chemical, usually petrol or paraffin. It's invaluable if arson is suspected; arsonists use accelerants.'

Palmer looked around him at the concrete floor.

'Footprints?'

Frome laughed.

'Loads, but mainly great big size eleven fireman boot prints I'm afraid. We have taken photos, but I don't hold out much hope there either. But you never know. We will run them through SICAR.'

He looked at Gheeta expectantly as he said this. Gheeta laughed.

'I know that one. Shoeprint Image Capture and Retrieval, a database of three hundred brands of shoes, trainers and other commonly worn footwear, and over two thousand different sole patterns.'

Frome was impressed.

'When would you like to be transferred to my department?' he joked.

Palmer ignored him, opened the cab door and looked inside.

'They torched the cab as well. Very professional job, very professional.'

He walked back to the rear doors.

'Whoever those poor three chaps were, they must have really, really upset somebody in a big way to end up like that.'

'Or perhaps they knew something they shouldn't know, guv?' Gheeta added. 'Something that could hurt somebody badly if it got out.'

'That's a possibility. But why knock 'em off like this? Doesn't make sense. They could have been killed in prison, much easier to have it done in there. If they were killed because they knew something that they shouldn't have known, it would seem that knowing it inside the prison was okay, but no way was it okay to get to the outside world with that information. I think this is going to be an intriguing case, Sergeant. Right, nothing we can do here so I think we will call it a night and see what the reports tell us in the morning. There's a take-away down the road, fancy some barbecued ribs?'

Gheeta's look of disdain said it all.

****

CHAPTER 3

Earlier on that afternoon, Harry Shore's mobile phone rang as he was studying the odds on a slip in a betting shop off Praed Street, Paddington.

'Shit!'

Quickly he filled in the slip and passed it with a twenty-pound note under the counter grille to the assistant behind.

'Twenty on the return favourite, Cheryl. Gotta take this,' he said, waving the phone at her. 'Expecting news from Peter's court case. If I win, I'll take you for a beer.'

Cheryl smiled benignly.

'That's a big *if* the way your luck's been running lately, Harry.'

She stamped the slip in her machine and passed him back the code number it issued.

'And it'll take more than a beer to get my knickers off.'

'That's not what I heard.'

They both laughed and Harry Shore hurried out of the betting shop to take the call on his mobile. He moved to the kerb out of the way of the shoppers wandering along the busy high street and took the call.

'Hello?'

'Harry?'

'Yeah, who's this?'

'Harry Shore?'

'Yeah.'

The line went dead.

A motorbike pulled up to the kerb beside him. The pillion rider pulled a Glock 26 pistol from inside his leather jacket and shot Harry Shore in the heart. Harry Shore was dead before he hit the ground, but another shot was sent into his head to make sure before the bike and passenger sped away, weaving through the traffic.

****

That evening, Frank Alexander stood looking out of his floor-to-ceiling office window on the 16th floor of the Shard on London's South Bank. He looked down on London Bridge and the commuters and tourists going about their business.

Fifty-six year-old Frank was 'numero uno' in the Alexander crime family, 'numero uno' because he was the last of the family; his father and uncles were all deceased, and his only brother had been killed in a hit-and-run ten years previously. A South London crime family, the Alexanders had built their empire up over four generations, starting with contraband and forged ration books after the Second World War, then into cheap stolen petrol during the rationing years, and then armed robbery of all types in the pre-CCTV days. Frank and his wife Gail used their heads to turn things into a legitimate business over the last ten years, as he could see the future of 'big reward' crime was in drugs and he wanted no part of that, unlike his brother who had tried to muscle in and had paid the price. The old-style East End and South Bank gangs had long been eclipsed by powerful, rich and violent Russian and Romanian gangsters, to whom killing an adversary was common place in their own countries and they had imported that criteria with them to the UK. Now Frank owned petrol stations and posh pawn shops, and only moved into criminal circles when the payout was so high as to justify the risk. Of course the business all looked straight and above board, with the correct accounting and auditing trails for any nosy HMRC inspector who took a look, but all was still supported to a large extent by illegal methods.

The petrol for the twenty petrol stations was forty percent stolen; honest tanker drivers working for the main suppliers and supermarket companies didn't put up much resistance when masked men with guns appeared beside them after a meal break at a motorway service station. Later, the tanker – now empty – would be found with the blindfolded and trussed-up driver safe in the cab a hundred miles from where it was stolen, the petrol already transferred to a blank tanker in the middle of nowhere and on its way to be pumped into the tanks at one of Frank Alexander's outlets.

The posh pawn shops were situated in the affluent parts of the main UK cities. It was easy money: those people who could afford the designer handbags and works of art were so afraid that their circle of elite friends would drop them like hot coals when things went financially wrong that they would accept almost anything for their expensive goods in order to keep up appearances. Alexander's high interest rates on the loan provided to them made it difficult for the client to redeem the goods, and so they often passed the redemption date and then off they went to a high-class auction. A Gucci bag worth five thousand pounds retail would be pawned for five hundred on a three-month redemption ticket, with interest taking it up to two thousand pounds, and if the client paid it, then all well and good, a nice profit. If they didn't, then off it went to auction with a three thousand-pound reserve.

But the top end of Frank Alexander's empire was still the big money heist. Old habits die hard, and Frank wanted to go down in criminal history as the man who pulled off the *big one* – the real *big one*; bigger than Brinks Mat, bigger than Hatton Garden or the Irish Bank. And now, at last, he had his *big one* in his sites.

His thoughts were interrupted as the door opened and his right-hand man George East entered. East was younger, in his forties, and had been with the Alexanders all his criminal life. He limped quite noticeably which was a result of a kneecapping given to him by irate IRA hierarchy when he and Frank's father mistakenly thought they could set up a cross-border petrol smuggling business between the Republic and Northern Ireland without asking permission or paying a percentage. East leant over and whispered something to Frank.

He nodded to East.

'Bring him in, George.'

East left and soon returned with a rather scared looking Robert Kershaw in tow. He pushed him down into one of the chairs and stood menacingly behind him, as Alexander walked round and sat on the side of the table alongside him.

'There's four people dead today because of you, Robert. Four people. Feel good about that, do you?'

Kershaw squirmed.

'I don't know what you're on about, Mr Alexander.'

'I'm on about your big mouth Robert, and the loose tongue inside it. Your little tête-a-têtes with your cell mates inside the Scrubs Remand Block, telling them that you were up for a big job, a Frank Alexander job – *my* job, Robert; the job *I* put together, Robert; my big finale. All ready to go, and then you decide to have a poke at a Post Office for pin money with your stupid mate Shore and get caught. What a fucking twat you are.'

Frank Alexander wasn't given to using such language, but the job he had planned was going to be the highlight of his career. The one that others would talk about for years to come; his personal Brinks Mat, his own Great Train Robbery. His anger got the better of him and he slapped Kershaw hard.

'I told you to keep your fucking head down and stay quiet, and out of the Met's radar, didn't I? I even gave you five grand upfront. So what do you do? You blow a fucking Post Office, get caught, and then broadcast to all and sundry in the remand cells that Frank Alexander is planning a big one.'

Kershaw was getting a bit worried about his own good health.

'I never said much. I don't know much, do I? I don't know what the job is, do I? You never told nobody what it is.'

'No I didn't, did I? And just as well I didn't, with big mouths like you on the team.'

'And what do you mean that there's four people dead because of me? How come?'

'Peter Shore, your cell mate for one.'

'Dead? Peter's dead?'

'Yes. I had a visit from his brothers George and Harry; they came here a fortnight ago and told me they knew I was planning a big job and they wanted in. Now, how would a couple of petty car thieves like them know about the job, Robert? I'll tell you how; they knew about it because brother Peter, your cell mate, had heard all about it from your big mouth and told them.'

'How come he's dead? George sprung him and Alli from the prison van with me.'

'No I didn't, Robert,' said George. 'Oh no I did not. If you remember you had a sack put over your head as you were hauled off that van. You didn't see the other two get off, did you?'

The light was beginning to shine in Robert Kershaw's brain.

'They're dead, aren't they.'

'Yes'

'Fuck's sake, Mr Alexander. Alli didn't know anything about the job.'

'Of course he did, he was in the same remand cell. He would have heard you and Shore talking.'

'Kept himself to himself. I liked Alli,'

'Well now you've got his death on your conscience, haven't you?'

'Who's the others then? That's only two.'

'I told you, Peter Shore's brothers Harry and George came to see me.'

'Jesus!'

Alexander walked over to the large window and stood with his hands in his pockets, gazing down over London Bridge as he spoke.

'George Shore thought it was just another day when he went to his lock-up this morning. He didn't know it was to be his last one, and all because of your big mouth.'

George East leant in close to Kershaw's face.

'If it was up to me, I'd have whacked *you* and your big mouth as well.'

Frank Alexander turned and smiled at Kershaw.

'Fortunately for you Robert, we need you because your brother-in-law Fred is in my plans for the job, and you are my only way of getting to him. Otherwise, George here would have had his wish.'

'Fred? What do you need him for? He's straight, never done nothing wrong in his life?'

'He's a security guard at the Royal Mint in Wales.'

Kershaw fell silent for a few moments.

'Fuck me, we're going to rob the fucking Mint.'

'Not quite Robert, but near.'

****

CHAPTER 4

By mid-morning the next day, the Metropolitan Police Serial Murder Squad's team room was busy; very busy.

Claire, the civilian assistant to the team, was handing out mug shots of the deceased, together with their potted criminal histories and known associates to the team of twelve detectives that Palmer had called in for the case. DS Singh was sorting out a number of iPads and their chargers for the team to take and use; they were programmed to use an encrypted intranet mail app that came directly into the servers in the Team Room, bypassing the Met's Communication Room to save time and maintain security.

Other cases the team were dealing with had been put on hold or downgraded as 'non-urgent' when the facts of this triple murder had become known to the 'suits' on the fifth floor at New Scotland Yard. The 'suits' had made it known to Palmer's immediate boss, Assistant Commissioner Bateman, that this case must be solved, no 'ifs', no 'buts'; Her Majesty's Government could not have prisoners murdered while in its care, and certainly not by a hitman or hitmen.

Bateman had passed on the instruction to Palmer by internal phone. Palmer had pointed out to AC Bateman that several prisoners inside H. M. Prisons were killed each year by other prisoners while in the care of her Majesty's Government, but Bateman had ignored that.

'Just get this one sorted Palmer, that's all.'

Palmer knew the real reason the fifth floor was getting twitchy on this one was that there was an election coming up, and the current Home Secretary and his Party were always assumed to be 'tough on crime'; a blatant unsolved serial murder would give the opposition a great deal of ammunition to question that assumption.

****

Palmer walked across the corridor from his office into the Team Room and looked around; it gave him a great deal of confidence as he recognised the faces of tried and trusted officers he had used before. On big cases like this one, he was able to pull in officers from other CID departments that were on leave or on days off to augment his team, which was basically himself, Singh and Claire. They all had the choice of not coming in, but it was usual to get a hundred percent turn-out; they liked Palmer.

He stood behind the main desk and clapped his hands for silence.

'Gentlemen, welcome. Nice to see familiar faces, I hope you are all well and had plenty of sleep, because as usual when working with me you're not going to get much down time until we solve this case. Those above are very concerned that when three people in custody are killed so easily it may give the public the wrong impression; it might, for instance, remind them that the force has had a twenty-seven per cent cut in manpower in the last three years.'

Palmer was not averse to getting a point across when he could. The murmuring in the room showed many were in agreement.

'Anyway, *we* are still here, and *we* have a job to do. You have in front of you printouts of the victims' files, and I'm sure some of you will have had dealings with them in the past.'

A murmur in the room confirmed that many of the Team had.

'Right, pair up. First off, I want you to get your ear to the ground on our patch. I want to know what this lot were up to in the last year or so and who with; also I want to know about any rumours about any of them falling out with anybody else. I want to know what is so important that those particular three chaps were killed, what ties them together. We need to find that link. As usual, DS Singh will issue you with iPads to upload any information straight to the computers for our systems to analyse and collate.'

He nodded to Singh who started dishing out the iPads.

'All communication to be through DS Singh as usual. Names are what we want now, and plenty of them. You've no firm procedural orders as yet, so just dig deep into your contacts, lean hard on the grasses and find out what's going on. Whatever it is, I've a feeling it's big. Three hits don't come cheap; somebody has put up a lot of money to shut those guys up, and I want to know who it was and why they had to be shut up. Okay, that's it – off you go. Any information we get coming in will be forwarded to you by Claire as soon as we get it, so keep your iPads on and take care.'

The Team sorted themselves out into pairs and left the room. Claire pinned three mugshots of Kershaw, Shore and Kalhoud onto the large white progress board on the far wall, leaving plenty of space for arrows and information to be written below each one as it came in. Palmer walked over and stood looking at it as Singh joined him.

'So you think they knew something they shouldn't have known then, guv?'

'Without doubt Sergeant, it's the only answer. You only kill three people if they know something so damaging that they have to be silenced, and silenced permanently.'

'So they could have stumbled on something whilst inside the remand centre?'

'Undoubtedly that's where they got it; that's the only place they could have got it.'

'Shore and Kershaw did the Post Office job together; they could have been in the know before they went down, guv.'

'No, if they'd ruffled somebody's feathers before they were nicked they'd have been whacked then. No, it's got to be something they discovered while inside – something about a past crime, or about a job planned for the future. But to kill them in order to silence them means it must be a bloody big job.'

'Sir!' said Claire, in a *stop everything this is important* tone. They both looked towards her.

'The pathologist's report has come through.'

She pointed at her screen.

'The third body wasn't killed *in situ* – that is, in the van – he was shot somewhere else and put in the van later; he was dead before he was put there. Bullet in the head same as the other two, but the bone fragments from the entry wound were not complete; the body had been moved about and lost some. If he'd been shot where he was found in the van, all the bone fragments would be there.'

Palmer barely had time to take this on board before a puffing Reg Frome came quickly into the room, quite out of breath. Without his all-covering white forensic paper suit and head gear on, Frome bore a distinct resemblance to Doc from the film Back To The Future; a shock of hair stood up from his head as though an electric shock had hit him, and a general unkempt appearance completed the *mad professor* look. But appearances can be deceptive; Reg Frome was a forensic expert of international standing, and was often called upon by Interpol for his input into difficult cases. It was Frome's forensic advances in DNA profiling that had led to the Hague trial and conviction of Madjik for the Bosnia genocide.

'Why is it that every time I want to use that bloody lift it's stuck on the fifth floor?'

Palmer smiled.

'Executive power, Reg. Has to be kept ready in case one of the Assistant Commissioners wants an early night. Any case, what brings you up here so soon?'

Frome placed his portly frame thankfully onto a chair and thrust a piece of paper towards Palmer, who took it.

'No doubt you've seen the pathology report on the third body? Well, I can tell you it was not Robert Kershaw – he was *not* in the van. The third body was George Shore, brother of Peter. We did a DNA test against the DNA library, and that's what came up.'

'Hang on, Reg, George Shore couldn't have been in that van. He wasn't on trial at Southwark,' said Palmer.

'George Shore wasn't *listed* as being in the van Justin, I grant you that. But George Shore was definitely the third body in that van, no doubt about it. DNA doesn't lie.'

'So where's Kershaw then?'

DS Singh took out her mobile.

'I'll call Southwark Court and get the CCTV from the backyard where they load the vans. We'd better make sure it was Kershaw who was put into that van.'

****

It was. Confirmation soon came back, as did an email file copy of the CCTV footage showing Kershaw, Peter Shore and Kalhoud being put in the van. This was quickly followed by a call from one of the team on the street, telling them that Harry Shore had been shot dead outside a betting shop the day before.

'Well, well, well, that throws a new light on things, doesn't it?' said Palmer, rubbing his chin thoughtfully. 'The whole Shore family taken out, and Kershaw apparently kidnapped.'

'The Shore brothers must have upset somebody in a big way,' added Gheeta as she pinned the headshots of George and Harry next to their brother on the progress board, and moved Kershaw's a little away from them. Palmer looked at the board.

'They certainly upset somebody, and that *somebody* needed Kershaw in a big way too. But why bother to put George Shore's body into the van?'

Gheeta shrugged.

'Maybe they thought the fire would destroy all his DNA, and we'd go on thinking it was Kershaw and not go looking for him?'

'Could be. Forensics say the same gun was used, so the killer or killers might have thought they'd fool us. But why not just spring Kershaw? Why all this killing?'

'We'll get the update out to the team, guv. I take it we are now looking for Kershaw as a missing person?'

'Yes, put his picture out. Don't bother with the Border Agency; I think this has all the hallmarks of a domestic squabble.

****

CHAPTER 5

'Three bodies all incinerated, and another shot in the street!'

Mrs P. was serving up Palmer's dinner in the kitchen at home that evening as he sat on the bottom of the stairs in the hall and prised off his shoes, watched by Daisy the dog who was hoping he'd pull a treat out of his pocket for her. No such luck.

'Oh, that is nice,' he said as he wiggled his toes.

'I don't think four bodies is very nice at all.'

'No, not that. It's nice to get my shoes off. About time we had a decent carpet in the room at work, instead of that cheap government issue rubbish that makes my feet ache.'

He gave Daisy the dog a pat and wandered into the kitchen.

'What's that?' he said, pointing to his plate on the table.

'Tuna salad with new potatoes.'

'I thought we were having toad in the hole tonight?'

'We were, but Benji borrowed the sausages.'

'Borrowed them? How can you borrow sausages?'

'He's had a new barbecue installed and wanted to test it.'

'I noticed all the smoke in his garden when I drove in the front. I thought he was having a bonfire.'

Benji – real name Benjamin – was Palmer's neighbour and nemesis: mid-sixties, ex-advertising executive on a massive pension, and nothing to spend it on except cruises and new big boys' toys; with a new expensive car every year – top of the range, of course – a non-fading suntan, a ponytail, and a mincing walk that Palmer had his suspicions about. But worst of all, the good ladies of Dulwich – those of a certain age, anyway – who used to have Palmer as their local hero to flirt and be cheeky with, had now turned their attentions to Benji; even more so after he was recently elected to the Local Council.

'He said he'd replace them.'

Mrs P. put the mayonnaise on the table and sat down opposite him.

'Replace what?'

'The sausages.'

'Probably be vegetarian ones if he does, all nut and hedgerow. He could have walked down the road to the shops and bought some for his barbecue.'

'The installers were waiting to test it. It's propane gas.'

'Gas?'

'Yes, four gas rings that heat some large stones, and then the heat from the stones comes up through the grill and barbecues the food.'

'That's not a barbecue, that's a gas oven. A proper barbecue burns charcoal; that's what flavours the food. Won't get much flavour off of hot stones.'

'It's the modern way. Eat your food.'

'It's a gas oven. Might as well cook the food in the oven in the kitchen and bring it out on plates'.

'Anyway, he's invited us round on Saturday for the christening.'

'Whose christening?'

'The new barbecue's christening; most of the WI are going with their husbands, and a lot of the councillors will be there too.'

'I'm working.'

'No you're not, you never work Saturday nights – especially if Barcelona are on

Sky. Wild horses couldn't drag you from the telly. How's your meal?'

'Horrible. I keep thinking of my sausages being mistreated on Benji's hot rocks.'

'Well you can question him yourself, he's just come in the back gate – and be civil.'

She nodded through the window as Benji approached it and gave them a wiggle-finger wave, before coming in through the garden door.

'Hello both. I thought I saw your car Justin, so I bought some sausages. I *stole* yours, did Mrs P. tell you?'

'She did, yes.'

'Here you are then,' Benji said, placing a pack on the work surface. 'Can't let you starve.'

'Vegetarian?'

'Of course. Linda McCartney's, tofu, nut and... something else I can't remember.'

'Hedgerow.'

'I do like your tee-shirt, Benji,' said Mrs P., hurriedly changing the subject and giving Palmer a glare.

'Do you?'

Benji beamed and opened his jacket to reveal a 'Harry & Meghan' photo tee-shirt.

'It's their wedding next week, so I thought I'd celebrate it at the barbecue on Saturday.'

Palmer nearly choked on his tuna.

'I'm definitely working.'

Benji was disappointed.

'Oh that would be a shame, Justin. Being a sort of official person, I had you in mind to propose the toast to the happy couple.'

Mrs P. stepped in as Palmer was about to reply with his usual diatribe about the *'family of pariahs that live at the end of the Mall'*.

'Justin has a very difficult case on at present, Benji. A quadruple murder.'

'Oh, how awful! Well never mind, you must come around one evening and I'll cook you a Benji special. I've a couple of my special kebabs on the grill right now.'

Palmer pointed out of the window at thick white smoke billowing around outside.

'I think they might be done, Benji. Either that or my fence is alight.'

A look of complete panic overtook Benji and seemed to root him to the spot, staring out of the window.

'Hadn't you better go and see what's happening?' Mrs P. suggested.

'Oh my god! Yes, yes.'

And he was gone. Mrs P. sighed and fixed Palmer with one of her '*I give up on you*' looks.

'One day, Justin Palmer, I won't be around to step in and prevent you from saying something in front of the wrong person that will backfire on you and give you a much-needed kick up the bum. You are a Detective Chief Superintendent, and need to remember that – non-political at all times.'

'The policing bill for that wedding will be about six million quid – and the taxpayer will pay it! Amazing how the government can find that while cutting the police budget every year, safe guarding their future knighthoods.'

'Enough! Most of the lower ranks would have been glad of the overtime.'

'If the government paid coppers a decent wage to begin with, they wouldn't need overtime.'

'Enough!'

Palmer was about to continue when the look on Mrs P.'s face made him reconsider and get on with his tuna salad.

****

CHAPTER 6

The next morning Palmer, Singh and Claire were in the Team Room going through the messages sent in by the team. They weren't very encouraging messages; no word on the street as to who was involved in the killings, no sign of Kershaw, and no whispers of a big job in preparation. It seemed to be business as usual in the criminal section of the economy. The one good thing happening overnight was that the prison van driver and guard had been found alive and well, after being driven out into the middle of nowhere in Lincolnshire and padlocked to a field gate. There they had remained, until a lady having a morning hack on her horse had found them.

'They are having a check-up at the local hospital, and as soon as the doctors give the okay I'll get them brought down here and see what they have to say,' said Gheeta.

'I don't think it will be much,' said Palmer. 'This is a professional job, I doubt whether they would have been allowed to see or hear anything of use. But have a chat with them, you never know.'

Lucy Ross from Press and Media Department gave a perfunctory tap at the door as she walked in, a sheaf of papers under her arm.

'Good morning all.'

She crossed to join Palmer and Singh as they returned her greeting.

'Oh, I see you have the case I want to talk about up on the board.'

She stood and looked at the progress board.

'Ugly bunch, weren't they?'

'Their mothers loved them,' Palmer said as he eyed the sheaf of papers suspiciously. 'I hope that's not all for me.'

'No, not all of it. I've just been in with Bateman; we are getting a lot of calls on this case from the press Justin, a bloody lot seeing that as far as I am aware nobody's tipped off the press about it. But they're on the scent and baying for details.'

Palmer shook his head.

'Not us, Lucy. We haven't said a word, but I've got a full team out on the street banging heads for information, so no doubt the press put two and two together.'

'Probably. Anyway, Bateman wants you to handle a press briefing as soon as I can get it organised; pour some oil on choppy waters, calm it down a bit.'

'I don't do press briefings Lucy, you know that. Bateman does them – he loves them; standing there in his smart uniform, making out he's in complete control when if the truth be known he hasn't the faintest idea what's going on.'

The three ladies smiled, knowing that Palmer's description of Assistant Commissioner Bateman's press briefings was just about spot on.

'I've put you in the frame for this one, Justin; in fact, I have insisted you take it. The murder of three prisoners in a prison van, and the brother of one of them gunned down in the street, and no arrests so far is going to generate a load of negative headlines about lack of security and no police presence on the street; all the usual stuff the media likes to hit us with.'

'No, let Bateman do it. He likes the limelight, he can give the *everything under control and arrests imminent* crap that he gives every time.'

'He would do it, but *I* don't want him to. I want *you* doing it. The press know you and your record, and it will give them confidence that we really are in control if they know you are at the helm. They know Bateman and his stock answers too well; they'd roast him and then us in print and on the telly. I need this one to come from the horse's mouth. I'll arrange it for midday in the media suite so we get the one o-clock news. Don't be late.'

She gave Palmer a wide smile and left. He looked from Gheeta to Claire and shrugged.

'Nothing like being thrown to the wolves, is there?'

****

Press briefings were one of Palmer's pet hates. He knew most of the press boys and girls, and over the years respect had been built both ways; he'd keep them up-to-date if they didn't make up their own scenarios or break his embargoes.

The briefing went fine; he told them what he wanted them to know, and didn't tell them what he didn't want them to know.

'Is it a gang killing, Chief Superintendent?'

'It could well be.'

'Romanian?'

'No.'

'Drugs deal gone wrong?'

53

'That's one of the scenarios we are working on.'

'There's a rumour the mafia may be involved.'

'No, there isn't any such rumour; you just made that up looking for a splash headline. Stop it – and anyway, I've had a word with Don Corleone and he says it's not his family.'

Laughter in the room.

'Is it true that the victims had been shot before the van was set alight?

'We are waiting for the forensic reports, but yes, they had been shot.'

'If it is gang-related, are we likely to see a gang war on the streets of London?'

'No.'

And so it went on, until the press was subdued and their hoped-for garish headlines about imminent gang warfare on the streets had been ditched in favour of ones about a drugs deal that probably went wrong.

Lucy Ross called an end as the questions dried up and whispered: 'Well done' into Palmer's ear as he left.

'Bateman would like a word with you.'

'Are you kidding?'

'No, a message came down just now. Perhaps he wants to congratulate you on a good press briefing.'

'I doubt it.'

****

'Well done Palmer, you handled the press very well.'

Assistant Commissioner Bateman smiled a false smile across his desk at Palmer sitting opposite. Bateman was the epitome of a social climber, but in the police force; he sucked up to anybody in authority he thought might assist in his career path to Commissioner. He was always immaculately turned out in a uniform with ironed creases that could cut bread. His nemesis was his head, in that he was bald, totally bald. It didn't worry anybody, except AC Bateman. It was hereditary: his father had been bald, his brother was bald, and he wasn't sure but he had a suspicion that his sister had started to infuse false hair pieces into her receding locks. He had once tried a wig, but the silence from all quarters of the Yard on the day he wore it, and the number of staff who kept their hand in front of their faces as he walked past put paid to that idea. Now he was contemplating a transplant and had a brochure from a Harley Street company on his desk, and was considering going for a consultation.

There had always been a distrustful undercurrent to Palmer and Bateman's relationship; nothing you could pin down, but Palmer didn't like or agree with fast-tracking of university graduates to management positions in the force. He'd have them do the two years on the beat first, see how they handled a Rastafarian drug dealer with a ten-inch knife who just did not want to be arrested. Bateman, on the other hand, would like to be surrounded with graduates with *'firsts'* in various *'ologies'*; he believed the old school coppers like Palmer were outdated dinosaurs, and that crime could be solved by elimination and computer programmes, which is why he had tried unsuccessfully to transfer DS Singh away from Palmer into a Cyber Crime Unit. Bateman had no time for an experienced detective's knowledge and experience being an asset, and the sooner he could shut down the Serial Murder Squad and combine it with the databases of the Major Crime Unit, CID and Cyber Crime the better.

The trouble was that Palmer's team, the Major Crime Team, CID and Cyber Crime were producing good case solve figures, which the political masters at the Home Office liked. But what really irked him most of all was that they really liked Palmer, the press liked Palmer, and the rank and file loved him. So he managed to keep the false smile on his face as he looked across his highly polished desk at Palmer. He had secretly hoped that the press briefing had been a disaster.

'Yes, went very well indeed. Unfortunately I was in an important meeting, otherwise I wouldn't have had the Media Department pull you in at such short notice.'

'That's alright sir, pleased to help you out. After all, it is my case so not a problem.'

'How are we progressing with it – any arrests imminent?'

'No, I'm afraid not. As you know we have a full team in the field, but silence reigns. Seems like three criminals have really upset somebody and revenge has been taken. I think Kalhoud was just in the wrong place at the wrong time and saw too much.'

Bateman nodded his head.

'Okay, I'll sign an order to release his body. He was Muslim, and they like to have their dead buried within twenty-four hours. How long will you keep a team in the field?'

'Just as long as I have to. Soon as we get a lead come through I'll stand them down.'

'Okay, just remember most of them are on overtime; got to keep the costs down.'

'I am sure most of them would rather have their days off sir, rather than be walking the streets of South London pressing low-level grasses to tell them the rumours.'

'Yes, probably. Just keep me informed and make sure I get your daily report sheets – preferably the next day and not a week later.

He rose from his chair, indicating the meeting was over. Palmer rose too and noticed the hair transplant brochure.

'Not another wig, sir? That last one didn't suit you at all.'

'No, not another wig, Palmer. I am considering a hair transplant.'

'Really, sir? Which one?'

****

CHAPTER 7

In the Team Room Claire was busy inputting the criminal backgrounds and the associates of the victims when Palmer and Gheeta came in, carrying a coffee each from the vending machine in the corridor. Gheeta had one for Claire and put it on the table beside her.

'Thanks', she said with a smile. 'Just what I need: a large caffeine boost.'

Palmer gave a sarcastic laugh.

'The only boost you'll get from that muck is an indigestion boost.'

Palmer liked his coffee fresh and percolated, and had an ongoing war with the vending machine in their corridor that had a habit of taking his money and sending the coffee powder, sugar, milk and boiling water down the tube before the cup. It only seemed to do this to him.

'How did the press thing go?' asked Claire. 'I watched it on the screen and it seemed okay.'

'The boy dun good,' said Gheeta in her best Cockney accent.

'Bloody waste of time,' said Palmer, crossing to the progress board while sipping his coffee and pulling a nasty face with each sip taken. 'Right then, all we can do is wait for some thread to emerge; a link to something that got these three killed. Anything in from the team boys, Claire?'

'Nothing yet sir, but it's still a bit early. Give them a chance.'

'Yes, you're right. A bit like treading water at the moment; lots of energy and going nowhere fast.'

Reg Frome poked his head in the door.

'Good afternoon all, just passing so I just thought I'd see if the TV star could give me an autograph.'

Gheeta took up the thread.

'Have you an appointment, sir? I'm afraid DCS Palmer has a very busy media schedule since his television success: he's off to Australia for *I'm A Celebrity Get Me Out Of Here!* and then straight into *Strictly Come Dancing*, and then onto the nationwide promotion tour for his new book. I can fit you in sometime in June next year?

'What about *Love Island*, isn't he doing that?'

'No, Mrs P. wouldn't let him go on that... She's going, but not him.'

Palmer gave them both a resigned shrug.

'All right, that's enough.

'By the way,' Frome said. 'I was in the Path lab earlier when they were doing a PM on Harry Shore; definitely a professional hit, one to the heart and a follow-up to the head. I've got the bullets and I bet they are from the same gun as the chaps in the prison van. I'll email a confirmation as soon as we test them. Must go – things to do, people to see.'

He nodded to Gheeta and Claire and turned to Palmer.

'Go on, give us an autograph. I was going to put it on eBay for fifty pee.'

And with that he was gone, before Palmer's expletive reply could reach him.

'And then there were four,' said Palmer, turning back to the business in hand. 'Have we had any statements through from the van driver and guard yet?'

Gheeta passed him a folder.

'Nothing of consequence, guv. They were pulled over by what they thought was a police car, blue light on top and uniformed officers inside; as soon as they opened the door a gun was pulled and they were blindfolded and taken off in the fake police car and dumped a couple of hours later, bound and gagged. I've got their CVs coming through from G4 but it doesn't look like they were part of it.'

'Okay, take a look and let me know if you think we ought to interview them.'

'Guv,' said Gheeta, 'I can't really understand this. I mean if you had a beef with the Shores then okay, knock them off. But why all the nonsense of putting George in the van and getting Kershaw out? '

'Only one reason, Sergeant: young Kershaw is needed for something. A hit, a robbery maybe, but whatever it is it's big; you don't knock off four people for nothing. Take a look at Kershaw's CR and see what his speciality is. I thought he was just a petty villain with a liking for guns, but perhaps he's got himself a trade, wheelman or explosives... Somebody needs him, and we need to know who and why.'

'But why kill the Shores? That was planned, they weren't just in the wrong place at the wrong time. They were targeted, guv.'

'They were, and we need to find out why. They've upset somebody, but how is the big question.'

'And who.'

'Yes, and who. Who thought it necessary to kill all three?'

'And Kalhoud?'

'He could be collateral damage; he could just have been in the wrong place at the wrong time. But he was in the same cell block as Kershaw and Shore so there's a link – a tenuous one, but we are grasping at straws at the moment so do a deep check on him too.'

'I got the rates office details about the warehouse back, sir.'

Claire set the printer working.

'It's due for demolition, a compulsory purchase by the council as part of the regeneration plan for the area five years ago. Been empty ever since.'

Palmer stood and stretched.

'Right, I think it's time we poked the hornet's nest. I think we might pay a visit to the Old Kent Road, Sergeant. There's somebody down there I think I need to renew my acquaintance with; somebody who I bet knows what's going on. Get your coat and have a car meet us at the front – we are going to the pub.'

****

CHAPTER 8

Gheeta had listened with interest as Palmer explained where they were going and why as the plain squad car made its way south of the river and down the Old Kent Road.

'Freddy Doorman is an old school 'geezer',' Palmer smiled.' Not a big player in the whole scheme of things, but not a bit player either. I first came across him when I was a young DC and seconded to Robert Marks's A10 unit in the late '80s. That was a special unit formed to clear out the corruption in the CID, and boy was there a lot of it! Marks once said that *'a good police force is one that catches more crooks than it employs'*. In that purge Sergeant, over 500 CID officers were sacked or resigned; quite a few went to Spain and bought villas next to the crooks they had protected and taken bribes from!'

He laughed.

'Anyway, Freddy Doorman's name kept cropping up and although we couldn't pin anything on him we knew he was a hitman and enforcer for the Krays and ran his own firm out of the Deptford and Greenwich area. It was alleged he was involved in the Cornell murder, but we couldn't get enough evidence; people wouldn't talk – wouldn't *dare* talk. Years later we finally got him as an accessory to the Krays in the murder of Jack 'The Hat' McVitie; the Krays' men had panicked after Reggie killed McVitie and dumped the body in a churchyard just south of the Blackwall Tunnel, right in Freddy's manor. When Reggie Kray heard that he phoned Freddy and told him; if he hadn't and we had found the body on Freddy's turf, we would have pulled him in and he wouldn't have been very happy with the Krays.'

Palmer laughed again.

'That would have been fun. Anyway, the body was removed and never found. But Doorman was implicated by a couple of grasses and went down at the Krays' trial for ten years.'

Their car pulled up outside the Walmer Castle public house.

'Come on, we're here: Freddy's office.'

The pub went very quiet as Palmer and the uniformed DS Singh entered. A few punters inside suddenly remembered they had things to do and left rather hurriedly; it reminded Palmer of what had usually happened in the 'old days' when police went into a busy pub.

'Well, well, well, Mr Palmer. Long time no see. What brings you to these parts?'

Freddy Doorman looked surprised, putting down his copy of the *Racing Post* and removing his glasses as Palmer and Singh walked through and sat down at his table in the saloon bar. Freddy's two minders stood up from their seats and looked to him for instructions.

'Just a social visit Freddy, don't worry. We haven't found the body.'

Freddy Doorman laughed.

'And you never will.'

He nodded to the two minders to go away and they retired to the bar.

'You're looking well for your age, Freddy. Still in the game?'

'Straight as a die, Mr Palmer. Everything strictly legit.'

'Leopards don't change their spots, Freddy.'

'I'm too old for any capers now, Mr Palmer; eighty-three, with a new hip and a dodgy knee. And a couple more stone than back then.'

He patted his ample paunch.

'Didn't stop your old mates Read and Perkins swinging down a lift shaft on the end of a rope at the Hatton Garden safe deposit heist, Freddy.'

'Yeah, bloody fools, and look where they are now: banged up and likely to see the rest of their days out inside a cell. That's not for me, Mr Palmer. Anyway, I see *you've* done well for yourself, *Detective Chief Superintendent* Palmer. Saw you on the telly too – three dead in a prison van, nasty.'

'Very nasty Freddy, and dumped right in the middle of your manor.'

'*My* manor? No, not anymore – I told you, strictly legit now. I've got a car sales pitch down the road with an old mate, and what with my state pension I'm okay, I get by. You don't think I want to fuck all that up, do you?'

He looked at Gheeta.

'Excuse the language, my dear.'

'I don't think *you* did it, Freddy,' Palmer said, smiling at him. 'But I think you know who did.'

'Not a clue Mr Palmer, no idea, I keep a thousand miles away from all that business now,'

'Really, Freddy? That's very good to know, 'cause I heard that some car sales fronts in this area might have a few dodgy high value vehicles on the books. You know the score: mileage clocked, and chassis numbers changed.

I'd hate for the DVLC chaps to target you, especially with you being strictly legit.'

The implied threat was not lost on Freddy. It had long been a police ploy to target car sales pitches that were suspected of 'ringing' stolen cars and inspect them on an almost daily basis, by DVLA inspectors going through paperwork and examining chassis numbers and making it almost impossible to carry on the illegal trade.

'I have a meeting to go to, Mr Palmer, if you've finished this social visit. I really must go. Here.'

He handed Palmer a business card from his inside pocket.

'Next time please make an appointment.'

'I've finished, Freddy; for now, that is. I've got a couple more old acquaintances of yours to visit in the area.'

He stood to go.

'Take care, Freddy. Things are going to get a bit hot round here until I get this case sorted.'

He nodded to Freddy and his minders and left the pub, followed by DS Singh. Freddy Doorman took out his mobile and made a call.

'Did you say we've got a couple more to visit, guv?' asked Gheeta as they settled back into the car.

'No, just planting a little bomb in Freddy's head. Here…'

He passed her Freddy Doorman's business card.

'Give Claire a call and get her to monitor that line.'

He checked his watch.

'It's 2.28pm now. I want to know the first number he calls now we've left, and who it belongs to.'

'You really think he knows about this caper, don't you guv.'

'He knows all right, and he'll get brownie points for letting whoever is running it know that we've been on the patch asking questions.'

He laughed to himself.

'In the old days, Sergeant, when a copper came onto the manor or into an estate they passed the word by banging a dustbin lid; now it's by mobile phone. Progress, eh?'

'Ah yes, but you wouldn't have known who was banging the dustbin lid guv, or who they were warning. With mobiles we can trace who made the call and who to – well, most of them.'

'And hopefully the call Freddy made when we left will lead us right to the killer's lair.'

'Don't bank on that, guv. In my limited experience of chasing criminals, things don't seem to happen that easily.'

She speed-dialled to Claire.

****

CHAPTER 9

'How big?'

Palmer looked at his two detectives who had been digging around in the Greenwich area. DCs Johnson and Simms were good; he'd used them before, pulling them into his squad from Rayson's East Greenwich CID when boots on the ground were needed.

'Pretty big, Chief,' said Johnson. 'But nobody is talking and even the usual *ton in the bag boys* are scared to chat.'

Ton in the bag boys was the name given to regular grasses who took a payment in a plain envelope for giving information.

Simms agreed.

'As soon as we mention the van murders, the silence is deafening. They don't want to end up barbecued.'

They were in the busy Team Room with DS Singh, Claire and the rest of his team, gathered for their Friday morning meeting to go over the week's work. Palmer stood up and called for silence.

'Right chaps, we don't seem to be getting very far. The whole underworld seems to have taken a vow of silence on this one, which means it's got a person or persons behind it that have a pretty nasty reputation of getting their own back on anybody crossing them. As you now know, Robert Kershaw was taken from the van and one of the Shore brothers put in his place. All three Shore brothers were killed, professionally killed. My own instincts tell me there are two reasons for this: one, Kershaw is wanted for some job coming up, and two, the Shores aren't wanted for that job. But why kill them? Only one answer to that as far as I can see, and that is to silence them; they knew what job it is and somehow they were in the way.

'Now, to kill three blokes to keep a job on track is a pretty big decision, so it's a bloody big job and I'll wager that it's a two-day job. There's a Bank Holiday weekend coming up in a fortnight, and I get the feeling that could be the time they've planned to do it; just like the Hatton Garden job, they need the time to get in and get whatever they are after, get out and get away. I may be totally wrong and it may be a simple armed hold- up, but something that quick wouldn't fit this scenario and this amount of protection.

'So, check all the specialist hardware suppliers on the patch you're covering; we need to know if anybody has ordered big drilling equipment, pulleys, protective clothing, industrial cutters, anything out of the ordinary. The other thing is to lean harder on your grasses; lean on any faces you know that worked with the Shores in the past, they may have dropped a hint. Go in hard, let them know that if we find out they've kept back information on four murders they'll go down for a long stretch.

'Now, I know it's the weekend and some of you will have made other plans, but any of you that carry on working the case will be paid overtime.'

There was laughter from the team. Overtime was banned with the government cuts slashing police budgets in all departments.

'Yes I know, but this case is top priority with the suits on the top floor and our political masters' reputations are on the line, so they will find the money. The media is just waiting to jump all over them for not putting the manpower in on a four murders case; as you know, I couldn't care less about the top floor or the politicians, but I do care about this department and both mine and your personal competence being questioned. You lot are the best in the business; if you weren't, you wouldn't be in here. So, if some thug or thugs get away with this one then there's not much of a future for any of us. So they are not going to get away with it, are they? Go get 'em.'

Palmer turned and sat down next to Gheeta at the computer servers, as the team left the room amid a cacophony of steel chair legs scraping on old lino and the hubbub of voices.

'Should change your name to Churchill guv, if you are going to give those sorts of speeches.'

'Everybody needs a little fillip sometimes Sergeant, and at the present time it's those officers. They put their lives on the line every day, and for what – a one percent pay rise in five years and to be treated like rubbish by those posh overpaid twats in government. If the thin blue line broke, I wonder who'd be first screaming for help.'

'Well the good news is that we've got a witness, guv. A homeless chap was sheltering in the warehouse when the van drove in and was torched. Just got a statement through from Rayson at East Greenwich who interviewed him; he's a known alcoholic, but Rayson says he's pretty reliable and has given good information to him before on drug dealers.'

'Anything worth following up?'

'It's interesting. He says the van drove in followed by a car, no description; two men in the van and one in the car; a body was taken from the car boot and put into the van, and a man with a hood over his head brought out of the van and taken to the car; then the van was torched and the lot of them left in the car.'

'What's so interesting in that?'

'The man who appeared to be in charge had a limp.'

'Really? Now that does cut the suspects down a bit. Not that we have any at present.'

'We have now, guv. Rayson says the only person he knows with a limp that could be involved is a chap called George East. East works for Frankie Alexander.'

'Frankie Alexander, now there's a name from the past.'

'You know him, guv?'

'I knew his dad, Ronnie Alexander; he was part of the Richardson gang. This case is like *deja vu*: first it's Freddy Doorman, and now the Richardsons. They had a fight you know, two eighty-five year-old ex-gangsters.'

'Who did?'

'Freddy Doorman and Eddie Richardson, last February at Thomas Wisbey's funeral. They had a punch up at the grave side.'

'Who was Wisbey?'

'One of the Great Train Robbers. You know about that, surely?'

'Yes, I saw the film. That was Ronnie Biggs, wasn't it?'

'Yes, Biggs made more out of selling his story and media appearances than he ever did out of the robbery. He was a small player; he was only in it because he knew a retired engine driver and paid the bloke a few quid to drive the engine after they'd stopped it. Trouble was, it was a new kind of engine and Biggs's mate couldn't start it, so they had to get the original driver back into the cab. Unfortunately they'd given him a wallop on the head, so it took time to bring him round and move the train to the bridge where all the transport was waiting. Anyway, that's all history. This George East chap seems interesting.'

'Shall I ask Inspector Rayson to pull him in for questioning, guv?'

'No, get Johnson and Simms to quietly sniff around; it's their turf. If something big is going down, then we don't want to frighten them off by feeling collars just yet. Get addresses for East and Alexander; with a bit of luck Kershaw will turn up at one of their places.'

He blew out his cheeks.

'But I still can't see what Kershaw brings to the party; he has no known criminal skills. We are missing something here, got to be. Run some deep checks on Alexander, East and Kershaw: known associates, habits, family, finances; see if anything comes up.'

'I've got the number back, sir,' called Claire from across the room, stood at the printer which was tapping out a page.

'What number?'

'The one Foreman rang when you left him.'

'Aha, well done. Whose is it?'

'Haven't got that, it's an unregistered mobile.'

Gheeta pulled open a drawer and took out a mobile phone.

'I'll try it and see what we get, shall I guv?'

'Yes, go on. Put it on speaker.'

They kept an unregistered mobile themselves, so that should they need to they could make a call that couldn't be traced back to the Squad. Claire came over and gave Gheeta the paper. Gheeta keyed the number in and held the phone a foot away from her with the speaker turned on. The number rang. After two or three rings, a male voice answered.

'Yes.'

'Hello?' said Gheeta.

'Who's that?'

'I was told to ring this number about a job,' said Gheeta.

'Who by?'

Palmer mouthed: '*George*'.

'George,' said Gheeta.

'George who?' asked the voice.

'*East,*' mouthed Palmer.

'George East,' said Gheeta.

There was long silence on the line, then:

'Is this a fucking wind-up?'

'No, why?' said Gheeta

'*I'm* George East, and I don't know you. Who are you?'

Palmer made a throat-cutting gesture with his hand, and Gheeta terminated the call. Palmer smiled a big smile.

'Thank you Freddy, you've led us straight to the middle of the web. Now all we have to do is untangle it.'

'So, it looks like Doorman was warning East about our visit then,' said Gheeta.

'And if East is Frank Alexander's number two, that means Mr Alexander is more than likely pulling the strings.'

'Inspector Rayson said Alexander would only be interested in something big, guv.'

'Something big enough to silence four people and kidnap one other. I think we ought to go and take a look at East; with a bit of luck, we might find Kershaw with him.'

****

CHAPTER 10

'My dad knew Palmer, he put him away once. Tough bastard.'

Frank Alexander sat at his office desk and pondered for a minute on the news that East had given him.

'He was one of Marks's 'young bloods' who cleaned up the Sweeney in the eighties; he wouldn't be nosing round here unless he had good reason to believe the murders were done on this manor.'

'Doorman reckons that was what he was snooping around for,' said East.

'Well, if he's snooping around for information it means he hasn't got much to go on so far, so we should be able to do the job tomorrow before they cotton on. Anyway, Palmer's looking for a gun and a murderer, not a big job going down. I take it you ditched the gun in the Thames?'

'No, can't do that – it's a rental. The bloke we got it from is coming down from Manchester for it next week.'

'Okay. Forensics will have matched the bullets with other jobs it's been used on in the past by now, so that will keep them busy.'

'I'll need the rest of the rental money for them next week. Five grand.'

Alexander laughed.

'After tomorrow night, George old friend, five grand will be mere peanuts.'

****

CHAPTER 11

The next afternoon in the Team Room it was quiet, unusually quiet with an air of expectancy. Surely things had to break soon? Claire was trying every avenue she could think of to find a link between the victims, but all that came up was their past criminal activities together. She went through all of those with a fine-tooth comb… nothing. Nothing was pointing to a reason for their murder.

In his office across the corridor, Palmer was going through the files he had asked for on Frank Alexander.

'He's a clever sod. A very clever sod.'

'Who is, guv?' said Gheeta, who was checking the reports from the team on the ground.

'Frank Alexander, he's as clean as a whistle. A very clever bloke… His dad was like that too. He was an original 'two stepper.''

Palmer had explained that term to Gheeta before when they had come up against an old adversary from the Brinks Mat caper called Harry James in the Loot case. A 'two stepper' was a clever villain who asked somebody else to arrange for something nasty to be done, and that person in turn asked somebody else again, somebody who had no connection with the original person, thus keeping that person two steps away from the deed and unknown to the final person who did the deed, and therefore unidentifiable.

'Something is going on in Greenwich, guv,' said Gheeta in an excited manner. 'Johnson has just texted that half a dozen known 'faces' have been gathering inside a snooker hall.'

Palmer stood.

'Get him on the phone and put it on the screen in the Team Room'

They both hurried across the corridor into the room as Gheeta speed-dialled Johnson. She spoke to him when he answered.

'Hold on a moment, I'm going to loop you into a speaker so we can all hear you and see what's happening.'

She put a jack plug into her phone and connected it through a modem on a server. The screen on the wall above it showed a busy Greenwich street.

'Okay, go ahead. The Chief can hear you and see the view from your mobile. Can you hear us?'

'Yes, loud and clear,' said Johnson over the speaker.

'What's happening?' asked Palmer.

'We had George East followed, sir. He met a couple of local faces at a café, and then the three of them came here to a local snooker club; it's one of Alexander's businesses so we pitched up outside to see what was next but they are still inside, and the local chap with us has spotted another three known lags go in as well. All six are better known for their muscle than their brains: club doormen and loan shark debt collectors. I've got the back exit covered but I don't want to send anybody inside on the pretence of playing snooker as we'd stand out a mile. And in any case, there's a chap on the door who is turning genuine punters away but letting the faces in. Simms buttonholed a punter who wasn't allowed in and apparently the chap on the door said it was an electricity failure and wouldn't be repaired until tomorrow. I'll show you on the phone's camera.'

The view changed to the club entrance.

'Can you see?'

'Yes, we can see him. They're obviously having a meeting in there or getting ready to go on a job. Is Kershaw in there, do you know?'

84

'Haven't seen him go in Chief, but he could have already been inside. Hang on... A cab's pulled up, can you see it?'

The screen altered as Johnson tried to get a picture of the cab's occupants, who were shielded from view by the cab and a bus passing by.

'Can you get across the road? We can't make out anybody.'

Palmer was growing exasperated.

They watched as the screen jolted around as Johnson slipped through the heavy traffic and crossed the road. Then it steadied as he held it up as though making a call with the lens towards the club entrance; two men left the cab and went into the club as it pulled away.

Palmer smiled.

'Frank Alexander and Robert Kershaw. Well, well, well, looks like the gang's all here. Well done Johnson, well done. Stick with it and let us know if anybody leaves.'

'Will do, sir.'

'Don't do anything other than follow them, understood?'

'Understood.'

'Good man.'

He nodded to Gheeta, who cut the link and removed the jack plugs.

'I wonder what they are up to. I don't suppose you've got a wonder beam amongst your box of tricks that we can aim at that snooker club and hear every word they are saying inside, have you?'

DS Singh's advanced knowledge of IT, cyber and anything technical never ceased to amaze Palmer. He was fully aware that some of the databases and websites she could access were strictly illegal, and turned a blind eye when they were used; as far as he was concerned, if it helped catch a killer then it was good to go, and two fingers to the human rights and politically correct numpties.

Gheeta laughed.

'I'm working on that one, guv. But I can access George East's phone and read any text messages he sends and see his photos.'

'How can you do that?' said Palmer, sounding slightly amazed.

'Well, you got Freddy Doorman's phone number and the trace on that first call he made after we left was to George East, as we know; so I got East's number, and using an American override system I can get into it and see everything. I get flagged up when he uses it, but so far he hasn't – not for texting or photos anyway. It's a bit like that big *News of The*

World hacking scandal a few years back, when they got into celebrity and royal mobiles and got the texts.'

'If memory serves me right Sergeant, the man from the paper who authorised it got seven years for that.'

'For what, guv?'

Gheeta feigned ignorance and innocence.

'For phone hacking, Sergeant.'

'Don't know what you are talking about, guv.'

The smiles they exchanged needed no words.

Claire turned with just as broad a smile on her face.

'I hope I'm not an 'accessory' to this. I was hoping for a fortnight in Madeira this year, not six months in the Scrubs.'

Gheeta's mobile rang again. It was Johnson.

'Okay… Yes, hang on. I'll ask the boss.'

She turned to Palmer.

'Johnson's got somebody round the back of the snooker hall and he's reported a large van has turned up at the back entrance, and it looks like the gang is going to leave in it.'

'Right, looks like we have some action then,' said Palmer, rubbing his hands together. 'Tell him not to do anything except follow the van, and don't lose it.' Then as an afterthought he added: 'Let me know if Alexander is in the van. If they're off to do a job, I bet he's not going with them.'

'Two stepper, guv?'

'Dead right, he's no fool.'

Gheeta relayed the orders as Palmer used the internal phone to order a plain squad car to meet them at the front. He rubbed his chin.

'I wonder where they are going – that's a fair-sized team for a small job. I reckon our Mr Frank Alexander has a fairly big one planned for tonight. I wonder where Robert Kershaw fits in as well; he seems to be getting priority treatment for a small-time thief.'

'Let's hope he doesn't end up like his mates in the prison van,' said Gheeta.

'No, I can't see that happening; not unless whatever it is he has that is making him so useful to them runs out.'

Gheeta's mobile rang again. It was Johnson. She plugged him into the speaker.

'The van has left with six of them in the back; Kershaw and George East have left in

88

a black BMW with a driver, and Frank Alexander has left on his own from the front of the building in a taxi. We are tailing the van in our squad car, and I've got Simms following East and Kershaw in another. We've no transport to follow Alexander, but I've got the licence plate. Ready?'

'Go ahead,' said Gheeta, as Claire picked up a biro and pad and gave her a nod.

'32HYX145, grey Honda CRV.'

Palmer was pleased.

'Good work son, good work. DS Singh and I are getting a car from the Yard and we'll get comms to patch us, you and Simms into one network, so hopefully we all end up at the same place.'

'Okay, sir.'

Palmer thought for a moment. Anything he'd missed? He didn't think so.

'Right then, let's go and get the show on the road.'

Gheeta thought he had missed something.

'We had better patch Claire into the comms too, guv. Never know when we might need some intel.'

'Yes, good idea Sergeant. Good idea.'

On hearing that, Claire's first thought was that she'd better ring home and tell her husband she didn't know what time she'd be home. Palmer had been bollocked so many times by Mrs P. for taking Gheeta and Claire for granted that a little bell rang in his head.

'Are you okay with that, Claire? Could be a late night.'

'I'm fine, sir. I'll let hubby know; he's used to it, so no problem. The check I did on the taxi number plate that Alexander is in shows that it's legally registered, fully licensed.'

'Good, that means we can check the driver's log and see where he drops off Mr Alexander. Right then, come on Sergeant, that car will be waiting at the front.'

****

CHAPTER 12

In the squad car they called Johnson and patched him in along with Simms.

'We are on the road now. Where are you, Johnson?'

'We seem to be heading west, sir. We've come over the Thames and are going west along the Embankment.'

'And you Simms, where's East heading?'

'Same direction, sir. On the A4 heading for the motorway.'

****

Palmer's car headed up to Hyde Park Corner and left along Knightsbridge towards the M4. Soon, all three were heading west on the M4.

Johnson called.

'Simms is just behind us sir, and East's car has slotted in behind the van in front of us.'

Palmer thought for a moment.

'Okay. Simms, drop back a hundred yards; keep back and turn off at the next exit, and go back and do a surveillance job on

Alexander's home. Claire will give you the address.'

'Okay sir, will do.'

'Where are you now, Johnson?'

'Coming past the Swindon exit, sir.'

'Oh, right. We are in front of you, so we will turn into the next services and let you pass us and tag along behind.'

Which is what Palmer's car did, and the convoy carried on west along the M4 as darkness began to fall.

'I'm getting hungry. Peas pud, and gammon…'

Palmer thought of the meal Mrs P. had told him was on the menu for that evening.

'You ever had peas, pud, and gammon, Sergeant?'

'Can't say I have, guv.'

'One of life's little luxuries.'

'You're easily satisfied aren't you, guv? Most people would want a big house, Ferrari, holiday home in Barbados and a million quid in the bank as their luxury, but all you want is peas, pud, and gammon.'

She laughed.

'With a sprinkling of vinegar.'

'Oh, now you are pushing it.'

'I don't ask for a lot, do I Sergeant?' he said, mocking himself. 'Where are we now, driver?'

'Coming up to the M32 turn off for Bristol, sir.'

****

The convoy sped past the Bristol exit and took the right-hand lane for the Severn Bridge. Palmer called the other cars.

'Looks like we are going over the bridge into Wales. No flashing warrant cards at the pay booths, takes too long to fill in the forms; pay in cash and stay undercover lads, please.'

'I bet we have to fill in forms to get the money back later,' Johnson said.

Palmer laughed.

'And in triplicate, Johnson.'

They all negotiated the toll booths, each car taking a different booth, and carried on behind the van and BMW.

'It's got to be a heavy job, hasn't it guv? I mean, as far as we know they aren't carrying weapons, so it would look like the bodies are wanted for moving stuff?'

Palmer nodded.

'So how does Kershaw fit in then? He's slightly built, not a bloke you'd use for physical stuff. He must be the key to the operation, that's the only answer that works.'

'Plenty of docks along the Welsh coast, guv. Could be something coming off a boat?'

'Yes, that's a probability. East was involved in a drugs gang in Manchester some time ago, and I have no doubt he and Alexander would be in that trade now somehow; that's where the money is these days. Maybe the men in the van are going to be used to unload something. Tiger Bay in Cardiff used to be a real smugglers' delight until they developed it, so I don't think it will be there; but there are many other little harbours and docks on this coastline.'

It wasn't Cardiff. The convoy sped past on the M4.

Johnson came on the radio.

'They are turning off, sir. Taking the B4264 signposted for a place called Pontyclun.'

'Pontyclun, that rings a bell.'

Palmer thought hard, until Claire provided the answer over the comms.

'It's the Royal Mint sir, it's just outside Pontyclun.'

'Jesus Christ! They're going to have a go at the Mint, the cheeky bastards!'

'Shouldn't we alert the Welsh police, sir?' asked Gheeta. 'It's not our manor,'

Palmer had a little inside smile at the way Gheeta Singh had picked up bits of Cockney slang into her vocabulary since joining his team.

'Yes, you're right Sergeant, not our *manor*. Best get a Welsh Armed Tactical Support team to meet us at the Mint. Claire, can you hear me?'

'Yes sir, loud and clear.'

'Good. Get hold of Bateman and explain what we think is happening, and ask him to contact the Wales force to assist us with an armed TS team. When they are on the way, patch them into our comms. Can you do that?'

'Yes sir, on it now.'

****

Assistant Commissioner Bateman was none too pleased to have his evening interrupted by the urgent tone of his pager screaming from his breast pocket; nor were his wife, the audience and members of the cast at the Haymarket Theatre where he and his wife were celebrating their fifteenth anniversary with an evening at the theatre. He scurried apologetically out into the foyer and saw it was from Claire, and called her back on his mobile where she brought him up to date.

The thought of a raid on the Royal Mint with Palmer involved did not sit well with him; the press backlash if things went wrong would put an end to any ideas he might have of career advancement. But, if nothing else, Bateman was a policeman, and a few phone calls later things were in place, with the Welsh force in the picture and a Firearms Team on the way to liaise with Palmer.

He conveyed as much to Claire, insisting he be kept up to date on what was happening in Wales, and settled down at the back of the theatre to wait for the interval, and Mrs Bateman's reaction to his disruption of the first half; a reaction he was not looking forward to. Bloody Palmer!

****

'He's turning off the B road sir.'

Johnson's voice came through loud and clear in Palmer's car.

'East's car is turning off, the van's going straight on.'

'Okay, you stay with him. We will stay with the van.'

Palmer took a deep breath.

'Where's he off to then?

'Llantrisant,' said Gheeta, who had been working feverishly on her laptop. 'Kershaw has a sister, Julie, who lives there.

'Explain?'

'I knew there was something familiar with Pontyclun, and then I remembered that when I did the family trace on Kershaw at the office on the BMD database, it listed a sister who lived in Llantrisant, near Pontyclun. I didn't pay much attention to that, as it didn't seem relevant to the case; I checked her out and she is clean: no convictions, married with a fourteen year-old daughter.'

'So what's Kershaw doing then – paying a visit? Popping in for a cup of tea?'

'No, Julie's husband Fred works at the Mint. I've been checking his surname Knoble against the Mint's HMR list and Fred Knoble is on it.'

'Right, so that's the plan; they've an inside man, Fred Knoble. Maybe he's a key holder and they are picking him up.'

He clicked on the radio.

'Johnson are you receiving?'

'Yes, sir.'

'Right, we think Kershaw has a brother-in-law in Llantrisant who may be in on this, so sit back and just watch. Keep us up to date.'

'Will do, sir.'

Claire came on the radio.

'Sir, AC Bateman has alerted the Welsh Force and they are sending a SWAT van who will liaise with you as soon as they are on the way.'

'Well done, Claire.'

The driver looked at Palmer.

'Getting near the Mint now, sir. Want me to hold further back?'

'Yes, but keep that van in sight, don't lose it.'

The Royal Mint's building came into view; a very large, very modern glass building lit up like a beacon in the night sky. It reminded Palmer of the Emirates Stadium, the Arsenal FC home, imposing and giving off an air of power. The road to the great front entrance was security barred, with steel risers in a line across it. The van carried on past and took a right turn into a narrow two-lane road, with high hedges along each side marked 'Deliveries'. Palmer's car followed with the lights out at a good distance. The rear delivery entrance was a large steel bar gate a good fifteen-feet high and twenty-feet wide, set on runners embedded in the concrete road. Behind the gate was a secure compound, and just inside it to the right was the gatehouse, a modern brick and glass affair; a security guard could be seen sitting inside.

The van pulled to a halt before it came within his view, and Palmer indicated his driver to stop as well. They were a hundred yards behind and pulled in behind a row of workers' parked cars.

The radio came to life with a Welsh accent.

'DCS Palmer sir, this is DS Rees-Jones of South Wales Police Tactical Support Group. We are on our way to the Mint, sir; twelve officers in riot gear and we have firearms if needed. We are in a plain van.'

'Nice to have you with us, Sergeant. I hope we won't be needing the guns, but you never know. The scenario is that we have a van of eight suspects parked up near the back delivery gate of the Mint, and we are parked about a hundred yards behind them. If you come up slowly with your lights out and stop behind us, we can monitor the situation from here.

'Will do, sir.'

The radio was busy.

'Johnson here, sir. East has pulled up outside a house on a council estate in Llantrisant, 28 Valley Road. He, Kershaw, and the driver are going up to the front door.'

'Okay Johnson, we have intel that Kershaw's sister lives there and her husband works at the Mint, so they might be picking him up. Stay watching and let me know what happens,' replied Palmer. 'Remember, we think East has a gun and we are up to four bodies so far, so no contact. Understood?'

'Yes, sir.'

****

CHAPTER 13

'Mum, Uncle Bob is coming up the path with two men.'

Sharon Knoble turned from looking out of the front room window with a questioning look at her mum.

'What? Are you sure?'

Julie Knoble was greatly surprised. She hadn't seen or talked to her brother Robert for three years; after his last criminal episode with a shotgun and a security guard delivering wages to a factory, she had sat down with him on his release from prison and told him to his face that she no longer wished to have anything to do with him, and to stay away from her family. So what the hell was he doing at her house at this time of the night?

The front door bell rang.

'You stay in the front room Sharon, and don't come out.'

She shut the front room door and walked down the hall to the front door, opening it and standing silently looking at her brother.

'Hello, Julie. Surprise surprise.'

'What do you want, Robert? I thought I made it very clear to you the last time I saw you that you are not welcome here.'

'We've come to see Fred, not you.'

'He's at work.'

'I know he is,' Kershaw said with a false smile. 'We are on our way to see him.'

'What for? He doesn't want to see you, and neither do I.'

She tried to shut the door, but Kershaw stopped her and pushed her back into the hall as he and the other two entered, closing it behind them. She flailed at them in a desperate attempt to keep them out, but a heavy push from East sent her backwards onto the floor. She screamed, and before she could scream again East knelt beside her and had a gloved hand over her mouth and pressed his face close to hers.

'No need for that. Just behave yourself and nobody will get hurt; carry on yelling and I'll knock you out. Understand?'

Julie nodded. East removed his hand and pulled her up on to her feet.

'What is this about? What do you want?'

'Good, that's better.'

East smiled as Sharon came out of the front room, looking terrified at the scene, and Julie pulled her into her arms. Kershaw smiled at her.

'Remember me, Sharon? Uncle Bob. We have a little job for you; you're coming with us to see Dad. Won't take half an hour, and then we will bring you safely back and go away.'

'You're not taking her anywhere, you bastard.'

Julie made a lunge at Kershaw, but East had been expecting it and brought the pistol from his pocket and cracked her on the back of the head. She hit the floor unconscious. Sharon was visibly shaking with fear.

'For fuck's sake George, that wasn't in order,' said Kershaw.

'She'll be okay. Get her trussed, or you'll get the same.'

The driver took a length of cord and some tape from the bag he was carrying. He and Kershaw tied Julie's hands and legs together before taping her mouth and securing her to a chair in the front room, while East held onto a sobbing and shaking Sharon.

'We'd better call 999 and get a medic round when we leave here.'

Kershaw was beginning to realise what he'd gotten himself into.

'This is way out of order. Frank never said anything about doing it this way. We was supposed to quietly take the pair of them in the car, not smack her about!'

'Then she shouldn't have got stupid and started screaming, should she?' said East, giving him a cold glare. 'I ain't going to let that stupid bitch ruin this job. You can check her out when we've done the job and brought the kid back; she'll be all right, I didn't whack her hard. Come on, we gotta get going.'

****

'They are leaving the house, sir,' Johnson reported in on the radio. 'Looks like they have a girl with them.'

'That will be the daughter, Sharon,' said Gheeta. 'What do they want her for?'

'No idea,' said Palmer. 'I thought they'd pick up Fred if he was part of the plan, not his daughter.'

'Fred Knoble is at work, sir,' Claire butted in on the radio. 'I've got the Mint's work schedules online, and Fred Knoble, 28 Valley Road, Lllantrisant is on shift tonight, six until two.'

'So what's with the girl then? Some kind of decoy?'

104

'Do you want us to follow them, sir?'

'No, we've got enough officers here to handle this end. Check the house; if Mrs Knoble is there, arrest her as an accessory and see what you can get out of her. But keep her away from any mobile phone; we don't want her warning anybody that we are about..'

'Will do.'

'The Support group is here, sir.'

The driver pointed to the rear-view mirror showing the large black TSG van pulling up slowly behind them. DS Rees-Jones, all in black, left it on the dark hedgerow side and joined them in the rear of the squad car. Palmer did the introductions.

'So, we really just have to wait and see what happens before we make a move. If we nab the lot of them now, we can only get them for going out with the intention to commit a robbery; if we wait until they actually do something, we can get them for attempting to commit one.'

Rees-Jones smiled broadly.

'Twelve months' probation for intention, or fifteen years inside for attempting. I'll go for the fifteen-year stretch, sir; after all, they have buggered up all our evenings at home, haven't they? Cardiff versus Swansea on telly tonight, my lads aren't happy to miss that. Somebody's got to pay.'

Palmer laughed. He liked Rees-Jones.

'How many of you are there?'

'Ten, sir.'

'Johnson to Palmer,' the radio announced.

'Go ahead, Johnson.'

'We are in the house, sir. Couldn't get an answer but the neighbour came out and said she'd heard a commotion and screaming, so we forced entry. Just as well we did. Mrs Knoble was tied up to a chair and unconscious, with a nasty bruise and cut to her head. She's come round now and we have an ambulance on the way. Apparently, Kershaw arriving was a surprise; they don't get on and she hadn't seen him for a few years. Anyway, the main thing is they've taken the daughter Sharon to the Mint where her husband works; he's not involved in anything with Kershaw and hates him, so looks like a hostage event is happening.'

'Right,' said Palmer. 'You hang on there until I can get the local force to take over from you, and then come to the Mint. But park up near the entrance. There's a delivery lane where the van from London has parked up near the main delivery gate at the back, and we are a hundred yards back out of sight watching it with the local TSG; so if and when anything happens you block off the lane. Understood?'

'Yes, will do, sir. Mrs Knoble wants to call her husband at the Mint, can she?'.

'No, definitely not. I want everything to appear normal here when East and his gang start their caper, so no phone calls. Understood?'

'Understood, sir.'

Palmer turned to Rees-Jones.

'Can you get a WPC and uniformed back up to relieve my chaps and secure the house? Be quicker than me going through the procedures, and I'll need them to get a statement from Mrs Knoble. Get her to hospital if necessary but stay with her. No phones.'

'28 Valley Road, Llantrisant,' Gheeta added.

'Got it,' said Rees-Jones. 'I'll do it on our radio, won't take long. Then I'll send a man up the road for an 'eyes on' what's happening at the delivery gate.'

Rees-Jones made to leave the car.

'Good man,' said Palmer. 'If East, Kershaw and the girl are heading this way, we all need to keep an eye out for them and get well out of view when they go past us.'

Rees-Jones smiled.

'They won't see my chaps, sir. I can assure you of that.'

Palmer gave a knowing smile to Rees-Jones; he had worked with TSGs before and knew how good they were. Rees-Jones left the car as Palmer picked up the radio.

'Claire, have you still got a signal from East's phone?'

'I have, sir. They are about half a mile from you.'

A minute or so later, East's car passed them and slowed to a stop behind the London van. East could be seen getting out, followed by Kershaw who had a tight grip on the girl. East opened the rear door of the van and said something to those inside, before he took hold of the girl and walked slowly behind Kershaw towards the gatehouse. Palmer noticed the TSG men pass along the path between the line of workers' parked cars and the hedge, barely distinguishable in the dark. Rees-Jones quietly opened the back door of the squad car.

'I think we know what they are after now, sir.'

'Go on.'

'There's a consignment of gold and silver ingots on the way from the Bank of England vaults. My AC contacted a Director of the Mint, and apparently it's the yearly delivery prior to pressing the annual commemorative coins for world-wide collectors, sovereigns and Krugerrands and all that stuff. About fourteen million pounds' worth of ingots in an armoured vehicle, with a Special Branch car following with armed officers. The Director has been told not to alert the Mint staff.'

'Right, so that's what East is after; it all falls into place now. No way could he rob that van with its armed escort, so he's going to get inside the secure compound and wait until the van's inside and the escort leaves, and then probably grab the stuff when the van is opened to be unloaded. That's got to be the plan; the blokes in his van are there to do the transfer to their van'

'But how are they going to get inside the compound, sir?' Gheeta asked. 'Knoble won't just open the gate and let them in, will he? Especially when he sees Kershaw.'

'No, not unless he is in on the job and his wife doesn't know.'

He turned to Rees-Jones.

'Get your AC to divert the armoured van and Special Branch lads to the nearest secure police pound; we don't need them here in case it all goes off. I'm assuming East has still got the gun, and we know he won't hesitate to use it.'

'Okay.'

Rees-Jones moved back as Palmer got out of the car, keeping a crouched position and wincing as his sciatica let him know he'd been sitting for too long. Gheeta followed him out.

'We will move up with your lads, and you join us when you've made the call,' Palmer told Rees-Jones, who disappeared away into the night.

****

CHAPTER 14

Fred Knoble raised his eyes from the crossword he was trying to master. A figure was approaching the gate out of the gloom.

Shouldn't be anybody around at this time of night... Could be one of the day shift come back for something they'd forgotten... Well, tough luck. Nobody gets in unless authorised, they should know that.

Once the figure was in the glare of the security arc lights, he recognised it. Robert Kershaw, the brother-in-law from Hell. His surprise soon gave way to anger; what was *he* doing here? Kershaw had been told in no uncertain terms by Julie that he was not welcome anywhere near the family. What was the bastard up to now?

Fred stood and pulled on his hi-visibility jacket. This was the last thing he wanted tonight; there was a secure delivery coming in soon, and he couldn't open the gate if any unauthorised person was around. Even the security staff at the Mint were never made aware of bullion shipments arriving; that information was on a very short 'need to know' staff list, so as far as they were aware it was a stationery delivery.

'What do you want, Robert?'

Knoble left the gatehouse, approached the gate and spat the words out.

'You are not welcome here or at the house.'

Kershaw stood ten feet from the gate on the other side.

'Hello Fred, nice to see you too. I want to come in for a chat, try to patch things up.'

'You've got no chance of getting in here, and even less of a chance of patching things up. Go away, before I call the police to remove you.'

'You don't want to do that, Fred. You really don't.'

'Don't I? Give me one good reason why not.'

East appeared into view from the side of the gate, pulling Sharon with him. She was obviously in distress.

'Is this a good enough reason, Mr Knoble?' East said in a menacing tone. 'Open the gate and your daughter is free.'

'What are you doing with Sharon? Robert, what's going on you bastard? Let her go now, or I'll rip your fucking head off you bastard!'

'Much easier to just open the gate, and then you do what you want Fred,' said East. 'Much easier.'

'I'm calling the police.'

Knoble turned half back towards the gate house.

'No you are not, Fred. Oh no.'

East kicked Sharon's legs away from behind and she fell to the ground screaming, as he pulled the gun from his pocket and aimed at her head.

'Open the fucking gate. NOW!'

Kershaw's mind was a jumble of surprise, shock, and anger all mixed in a whirlpool of emotions. The anger at seeing his niece in such a state took over.

'For fuck's sake George, have you gone mad? You can't do that!'

He lunged at East to wrestle the gun from him, but was not strong enough. East pushed him sprawling to the ground beside Sharon.

'You bastard!'

Kershaw started to scramble to his feet and East hit him hard with the gun and he fell back to the ground unconscious. Behind them the van door burst open as their gang of helpers heard the rumpus and panicked, spilling out onto the road like commuters from a packed rush hour tube train.

From the darkness between the parked cars and the hedge, Palmer had seen enough. He stepped out with the TSG in line behind him and shouted loudly: 'This is the police armed response unit. Stay where you are and put down the gun, East. Everybody put your hands in the air where we can see them. I repeat, this is a police armed response unit.'

The gang in the van who had been coming out fast froze, and their hands slowly went up as they saw a line of ten dark figures with rifles aimed at them. East had other ideas. No way was he going to give up, no way! He'd been inside, and he wasn't going back. He grabbed Sharon and hauled her up off the road, holding her in front of him, the gun at her head as he backed towards his car.

'Stay away, or the girl gets hurt!' he shouted back.

Rees-Jones whispered in Palmer's ear.

'I could take him down with one to the leg, or put him out permanently with a head shot, sir?'

'Christ no,' Palmer replied. 'Don't do anything until we have the girl well away from him.'

He shouted to East.

'East, you are making it worse for yourself, don't be stupid. You can't get away, so let the girl go and put the weapon on the ground.'

A sudden movement from the gate attracted everybody's attention. Fred Knoble, incensed by his daughter's terrified position, had come out through the small Judas gate used for gatehouse staff and was running at East. He got to within a few yards before East shot him in the leg and brought him down writhing in pain on the road.

'Don't anybody else try anything, or you get the same!' East shouted as he opened the car driver's door on the side away from everybody and pushed Sharon in, telling her to get over to the passenger seat which put her between him and the TSG weapons. The car started and sped off into the darkness.

Palmer was the first to get to Knoble.

'Where does this road lead to?' he shouted at Knoble, who moaned and groaned on the ground. Palmer hadn't time for sentiment.

115

'Oh come on Fred, you aren't going to die; but your daughter might if you don't liven up. Where does it go?'

'Back to the main road,' Knoble managed to splutter out as a TSG man wrapped a tourniquet round his shot leg. 'It joins the main road to the motorway.'

'Right.'

Palmer looked around. All was under control, with the gang members from the van seated on the ground with their hands cuffed behind them and watched over by TSG men. He hurried over to Rees-Jones.

'You take this lot in and find them cells for the night. I'm going after East.'

'Okay sir, no problem. Do you want any of my men with you?'

Palmer thought for a moment.

'No, I don't think so. East is a Londoner, so I'll bet he's on his way there to go under cover as quick as he can. Get a call out to the Motorway boys with a description of him, the girl and the car, they should be able to pick him up. But don't try to stop him, just report and follow.'

'Okay, sir. Good luck, and take care.'

'And get the operators of any surveillance cameras on the M4 or the bridge to watch too,' added Palmer as he made his way back to his car. 'Come along, Sergeant,' he said, beckoning to Gheeta. 'We've got an armed robber with a child hostage who has just shot a security guard and probably murdered four others, and he's got a start on us.'

He rolled his eyes.

'Going well so far, eh?'

They got into the squad car and raced off in pursuit. Gheeta tapped away at her laptop keyboard.

'We've got eyes on him, sir.'

'What?'

'As long as he keeps his phone on, I can trace the signal. Give me a minute and I'll overlap it onto a map.'

Her fingers worked the keyboard.

'There he is.'

She showed the screen to Palmer, which showed a road map with a flashing dot moving along a road.

'He's crossed over the motorway and is heading into Cardiff.'

'Cardiff? Why would he go there?'

****

CHAPTER 15

Frank Alexander was at home in his mock Tudor mansion that backed onto Blackheath golf course, and was about to watch a film on TV with his wife Gail as he waited for news.

'Shouldn't he have phoned by now?' Gail said. She was getting agitated. She looked at her ladies Rolex. 'It's getting on a bit.'

'He'll phone, be patient.'

'He might have done the job and buggered off with the loot. I wouldn't trust your mate East with a pound coin, let alone a van full of gold.'

This was all rubbish. Gail Alexander, ex-reality television star and 'no knickers' paparazzi magnet had seen the pound signs flashing when Frank Alexander had fallen for her. He was twice her age and twice divorced, and liked to have a nice 'bit of eye candy' on his arm at social events, most of which were held by the charities he supported in his quest to drop the *gangster* tag and become Frank Alexander respected *businessman*. So it worked for both of them for a few years, but then the rot had gradually set in; Frank became more subdued as the years passed and liked evenings in and the quiet life, while Gail still wanted the attention of her peers, the media and the false respect that money can buy. So more and more Frank asked George East to chaperone Gail on her 'girls' nights out'.

'Just keep an eye on her, make sure no toe-rag tries to step in.'

The toe rag who did step in was George East himself, fifteen years younger than Frank and on Gail's radar from day one. Their relationship blossomed into a full affair which George thought was love and Gail knew was just occasional sex. But it suited her; she could control East and the more he had become infatuated with her, the more she held out the false promise of a life together: 'If only I could get away from Frank.' And this Mint job had thrown up that opportunity.

Trouble was, she and East didn't know it, but Frank knew all about them. Frank also knew it was no good waiting by the phone biting your fingernails when a job was going down; nothing you could do now, and if the planning had been right the only call would be one telling him it had been successful, and he was now a much richer man. The mobile rang. He smiled at Gail confidently, picked it up from the coffee table and looked at the caller's ID. It was East.

119

'Good news I hope, George.'

The panic in East's voice set alarm bells ringing in Frank's head.

'Fucking joking aren't you? The law was waiting for us. Somebody grassed.'

'What? What happened?'

East ran through the evening's events. Alexander couldn't believe it.

'Jesus, George. You shot a guard, and now you're in a car with the girl hostage with every copper in Wales looking for you.'

'That's about it, yes.'

'Dump the girl, for fuck's sake get her out of the car. On your own you stand a chance of getting away, with her you've no chance.'

'Okay, but how did they know, Frank? How did the law know about it? Whoever the grass is, he's on borrowed time.'

'Nobody grassed, George. Freddy Doorman told you about Palmer's visit, he's traced that fucking gun to you and had you – and probably me – under surveillance. Ditch the girl in a town and get rid of the phone too; they've probably got the number somehow and can see where you are by its signal.'

'Okay, I'll get to your place as soon as I can.'

'Christ no, don't come here – this is the first place they'll stake out. And keep out of London. Ring me on the landline when you settle.'

'Okay.'

The phone went dead.

Frank looked at Gail.

'Shit!'

****

CHAPTER 16

George East turned off the mobile and put it in the glove box. He looked across at Sharon who sat hunched as far away from him as she could on the passenger seat, fear in her wet eyes.

'Right then kid, looks like we have to part company.'

He pulled up alongside a row of closed shops and brightly lit open take-aways.

'Out you get.'

Sharon didn't need telling twice, but she got out of the car slowly, watching East like frightened prey watching its attacker.

'Shut the bloody door.'

As soon as she did he was off, all the time checking his mirrors for flashing blue lights. He took the back road from Cardiff to Newport and headed up onto the motorway, pulling into the services. He had a plan. Parking the car, he retrieved the mobile from the glove compartment and walked slowly to the lorry park. He walked along behind a row of HGVs until he saw one with its side lights on, the driver getting ready to depart. Turning the mobile back on, East slipped his arm under the side tarpaulin and threw the mobile as hard as he could into the lorry, and then quickly went back to his car as the lorry roared into life and left the services, joining the M4 bound for London.

East also left and took the motorway to the second Severn crossing; he intended to get into Bristol and then to London on the A4 through Bath. He thought the police would be watching the cameras on the M4 motorway, so best keep off that.

****

CHAPTER 17

'He's back on, guv.'

Gheeta pointed to the flashing dot on her laptop screen. They had been worried when it went dead, but now it was flashing away going south on the M4.

'He must have been in a bad reception area. Looks like he's off to London.'

'Yes, that makes sense; home turf, that's where he can disappear fast,' Palmer agreed. He turned to the driver. 'Foot down, blues on, we need to catch him up.'

He flicked the comms on.

'DS Rees-Jones, are you still there?'

'Yes, sir. We've handed the prisoners over to uniformed branch, sir; they'll be split into two groups and banged up for the night in separate cells, in two different police stations.'

'And Mr Knoble?'

'He's on his way to hospital sir, and his wife is joining him there.'

'Good, just need to get their daughter back in one piece now. Just one more thing Sergeant, make sure we get the bullet from Knoble's leg; we can tie it to the gun and the gun to East, and no doubt it will match the bullets taken from the other bodies, which will put him in the frame for them all.'

'Will do, sir.'

'Good man.'

He turned to Gheeta.

'Now all we need to do is catch up with the bastard before he vanishes in London.'

Gheeta was thinking ahead.

'Do you want a couple of pursuit cars to join us on the motorway, guv? If we catch him and do a box-stop we'll need them.'

'Yes, good thinking Sergeant, and make sure they include armed officers and a dog handler. I'm not really worried if they shoot him if he uses that gun again; we've enough to make a copper-bottomed case on him dead or alive.'

'Tut tut, sir,' Gheeta said, feigning shock. 'Everybody has the right to a fair trial.'

'Save the taxpayer a lot of money on court costs if he gets one between the eyes though, wouldn't it.'

Gheeta gave a false sigh.

'But think of the paperwork, sir: referring ourselves to the PCP, triple reports and witness statements, you and I suspended until the PCP finished their investigation. Much easier to hand him over to the CP lawyers and let them do it all.'

'Yes,' Palmer said, resigning himself to the way of things. 'I know, but then he gets life and the taxpayer has to cough up seven hundred quid a week for the prison costs.'

'Dead or alive, the taxpayer loses, guv.'

She called up Claire to arrange for the pursuit cars to come on behind them at the Swindon exit. They crossed the Severn on the old bridge, and were soon speeding past Bristol.

'How far ahead is he now?' asked Palmer.

'Fifteen miles, sir; he had quite a start on us. I reckon we will be on him coming up to Reading.'

'Good. I'm getting hungry, are you?'

'Not really, guv. Peas, pud, and gammon calling you from afar?'

Palmer laughed.

'Probably in the dog by now. I think Daisy Dog likes it when I miss an evening meal; if it's not freezeable, she gets it.'

They picked up the two marked pursuit cars after Swindon, made radio contact and sped on. Five minutes later, Gheeta called an alert.

'We shall be on him any time now, guv.'

She pointed to the green flashing dot.

'That's him, and…'

She tapped at the keys and a red dot flashed behind it.

'That's us.'

'We are right behind him, aren't we?'

He radioed the pursuit cars.

'Looks like we are about to catch him, gentlemen: black BMW, male driver and a girl. He's using her as a hostage, so be aware that we don't want any accidents.'

Palmer peered ahead through the windscreen.

'Right then East, where are you?'

They raced on another three miles.

'Guv,' Gheeta said, sounding worried. 'He's showing behind us now.'

'Behind us? We haven't passed a BMW. He can't be behind us.'

'He could be if he changed cars.'

'Damn, I didn't think of that. Okay, all cars pull onto the hard shoulder and stop, hazard lights on.'

The three cars pulled off and waited as Gheeta watched the flashing dot approaching.

'Now! He's level with us now!'

Palmer watched the traffic; it was a lone lorry that was passing.

'He's in that lorry. He must have got a lift.'

'Or stowed away in the back, guv. Do we stop it or follow it to its destination?'

'We stop it. Once it gets into London traffic he could hop off and run at anytime. We stop it.'

He gave the order to the pursuit cars and they pulled back onto the main carriageway, turned on the sirens and blues and in no time had pulled the lorry over onto the hard shoulder. Palmer's car pulled up in front, and he walked slowly to the cab with three armed officers flanking him and another three stood at the rear of the lorry, their rifles raised. The driver leaned out of his window above them as Palmer approached.

'Don't tell me I've got a load of illegals in the back, I was checked out as all clear at Swansea docks.'

'Not as far as we know, driver. Anybody in the cab with you?' Palmer asked with a smile.

'No, just me.'

'Okay, step down if you would and I'll explain.'

The driver opened the door and stepped down. An officer stepped up and looked inside.

'All clear in here, sir.'

Gheeta had her laptop open and the dot was flashing.

'He must be in the back, sir.'

'What are you carrying?' Palmer asked the driver.

'Two hundred and eighty-two sacks of potatoes.'

'Okay, we think that a dangerous person who is on the run might have got inside at some stage, and we need to take a look. My chaps will lift the side flaps, but you go and stand well away; he may be armed.'

The driver didn't need telling twice, and hurried away to stand behind the far police car. Palmer waited for a break in the traffic, which had started to slow down as drivers became inquisitive as to what was happening. When a break came, he shouted an instruction into the lorry.

'George East, we know you are in there. Throw out the weapon and come out with your hands showing. I have armed officers surrounding the lorry, so don't be stupid.'

Nothing happened. Palmer nodded to the officers.

'Okay gents, let's open the nearside curtain. Slowly.'

One officer knelt on the ground below the lorry's floor level, reached up to slip the retaining hook from its eye and slowly pulled the curtain along, bringing a stack of twenty kilo potato sacks into view, six sacks high.

Palmer tried again.

'Come out East, or the dog comes in.'

Nothing. Palmer beckoned the dog handler forward from the car.

'Put him in please.'

Unleashed, the dog was off up onto the sacks like a streak of lightning. They waited, hoping not to hear a gunshot. Nothing happened for a short while. The dog re-appeared, tail wagging and looking to its handler for instructions.

'There's nobody on that wagon, sir,' the handler said. 'If there was he'd have barked a signal. It's empty.'

Palmer turned to Gheeta and raised his eyebrows. She showed the laptop screen.

'It's still flashing, sir.'

'Ring it,' said Palmer, realising what had probably happened. Gheeta used her mobile and keyed in East's number. Somewhere in the back of the lorry, a ringtone rang out and repeated itself.

'Sir,' an armed officer said, pointing into the sacks near the back. 'It's in here.'

Palmer joined him and peered between the rows of sacks where East's phone was lit up and ringing

'The crafty bastard, he dumped the phone in here. He must have cottoned on that we had the number covered.'

'He could have just turned it off,' Gheeta said as she joined him.

'He could have, yes; but by doing this little trick he had us going one way while he probably went the opposite. Damn... Okay, get Claire to put out a 'stop and detain' at all UK exits. Make it a red one, care needed.'

Gheeta went back to the squad car and called Claire with the order.

****

CHAPTER 18

George East pulled into the concourse at Bristol Temple Meads station and parked at the back of the parking lot. He left the car, and avoiding the CCTV cameras walked up to the drop-off point, blending into the busy crowd of travellers and commuters entering and leaving the station. He watched carefully as cars and taxis pulled up, disgorging their passengers. He was looking for his next mode of transport.

He didn't have to wait long. A dark KIA pulled into the kerb a few feet in front of him; the passenger was obviously the daughter of the driver, probably being dropped off by dad on her way back to university as the boot opened to reveal two suitcases. Dad and daughter both got out and went to the boot, each hauling out a case, and then Dad shut the boot. His cheery smile turned to a look of horror as his car moved away from him, down the concourse and onto the road with East at the wheel. Dad's big mistake was to have left the engine running as he emptied the boot – just what East was waiting for.

He drove off to the A4 and towards Bath and London. He stopped once just past Bath at a petrol station and filled up using cash, keeping his face off the CCTV camera at the pay-point. He hoped that it would be sometime before the car was linked to him. Why would it be? It was just another car theft for Avon Police to log and send out the details of; only when the car he'd parked at the station was found and matched to him would the details be sent through to Palmer and the link made. Plenty of time. He wasn't taking the motorway, so no Motorway Patrol car or CCTV cameras would make a hit with the onboard CPNR computers.

****

CHAPTER 19

Frank Alexander was waiting at his home for a second phone call on the landline. He'd dozed off a few times in the arm chair since East's first call, and Gail was asleep on the sofa. Time seemed to drag ever more slowly as the hours went by. He picked it up quickly when it rang at just gone four in the morning.

'I'm back,' George East announced.

'Don't come here,' said Alexander. 'They'll be watching the house. Did you ditch the girl and the phone?'

'Yes, I'm on a payphone'.

'Where?'

'Victoria. I ditched the old car in Bristol and blagged another one.'

'Dump it, then get a taxi.'

'Where to?'

'Not here. Go to the snooker hall, I'll get somebody to go down and open up the back for you. Did you get rid of the gun?'

'No, I might need it.'

'What for? You bloody fool, that gun will have been tied to all the murders so you don't want to be caught with it! Clean it and dump it.'

'I'm not going to get caught. That gun got me away at the Mint, I'll dump it when I'm clear.'

'What's your plan?'

'I need to go to my safe deposit box in the morning and get some cash out first; then speak to a few people and get out of the country.'

'I thought that box was your pension?'

'It was, but needs must.'

The phone went dead. Alexander turned to Gail, who was now standing beside him.

'Bloody fool's still got the gun.'

'I told you ages ago he was trouble,' said Gail. 'He always was. Now look at what he's done. Bloody trouble.'

'I'm in the clear. Nothing can be pinned on me, and I think it's time me and George East parted company.'

'How are you going to do that?'

'One phone call. But not a traceable one.'

He took a 'burner' mobile phone from his pocket and dialled.

East was not anywhere near Victoria as he'd told Frank; he was in a telephone box opposite the snooker hall in Greenwich. He left it and walked a good distance up the street before moving into the darkness of a shop doorway from where he could see the snooker hall. He didn't have long to wait until what he thought might happen did happen.

Silently, two unmarked police cars drew up a little way down the street from the hall and six armed officers got out and moved silently to the hall, two staying at the front while the other four disappeared into the alleyway leading to the rear.

East watched, and then moved quickly and quietly away from the area.

****

CHAPTER 20

The next morning Palmer stood in the Team Room, studying the progress chart and stifling a yawn. It was two in the morning when he had finally got home, and he had managed to grab a few hours sleep before coming into the Yard. Gheeta was already in, and seeing that she couldn't have got home much before him he was surprised at how fresh she looked. He put it down to age difference; he'd lost count of the number of times he'd looked at Daisy when he'd got home at some unearthly hour and said: 'I'm getting too old for this.'

Beside the progress chart Claire had pinned up a large map showing the road route George East and his gang had taken to Wales, and the route East had taken back again; it ended in London, which was just an assumption.

Claire and DS Singh were working at their keyboards. Johnson and Simms came into the room carrying coffees and joined them. Damn, they looked fresh as well. Palmer stifled another yawn.

'Where are you now, Mr East?' asked Palmer of nobody in particular. 'Where oh where?'

Gheeta broke off from her terminal.

'Not at the snooker club, that's for sure. Bit of a stitch-up that was, sir.'

'What was that?' Simms asked.

Palmer exhaled in a resigned manner.

'Your people at Greenwich had a call from an untraceable mobile last night saying East was at the Snooker Club. He wasn't. Rayson sent a TFG on a wasted journey.'

'Why would anybody bother to give a false lead?'

'Maybe it wasn't false when they phoned it in, but East left before we got there,' Palmer said. 'Or perhaps East himself rang it in while he went elsewhere for the night.'

'So if it wasn't false and he was there for a while, who called? Who wants East caught?' asked Gheeta.

'Yes, I've been pondering that myself. The main suspect has got to be Frank Alexander. The last thing he wants is to be implicated in murder; that would really dent his carefully built-up reputation as a clean businessman. But then again, it might well have been East himself, nicely tucked up with one of his mates in Manchester or Liverpool giving us the run-around'

Claire turned from her screen.

'The circumstantial evidence points to him being in London, sir. Have a look at this.'

She pointed to one of the large screens on the wall above the computers. It lit up with a map of the roads between Wales and London. A red line followed the M4 from Wales into Bristol.

'That is East's original car, picked up on the NRCs. Last seen on British rail CCTV parked all night at Bristol Temple Meads station car park, without a ticket so when the parking attendant booked it in it was flagged up as 'of interest' to us, and Avon Constabulary emailed the info through.'

'Did it pick up East parking it there?'

'Picked up a figure, but too dark to positively identify. He parked it well away from the cameras in a far corner of the car park.'

'Right, so East dumped it there and presumably got a train to somewhere? Get the station CCTV checked.'

'Not necessarily sir, no.'

'No?'

'Well, maybe he did. But a car was stolen from the station concourse at ten o'clock last night, twenty minutes after he arrived there. The driver left the engine running as he got

139

suitcases out of the boot, and somebody jumped in and drove off.'

'East?'

'Can't say for sure – no real description from anybody, it all happened very quickly. But, this is the route that car took according to NCRs.'

A green line left Bristol and took the A4 all the way to London.

'That is too much of a coincidence, isn't it? That has to be East.'

'We may be able to determine that, sir,' said Gheeta. 'If it was East then he'd be very careful not to draw attention to himself. He wouldn't want a patrol car to pull him over, so we have input a constant speed of 40 to 50 mph on the journey between each NCR. It all tallies except for one leg of the journey. This one.'

A portion of the green line flashed bright and dark.

'It's an eighteen-mile stretch between the two cameras and it took the car forty minutes.'

'Bit slow, isn't it?'

'Exactly, so we think he must have stopped somewhere for some time.'

Palmer got the picture.

'Petrol.'

Gheeta nodded.

'Or food. I've asked Avon and Wiltshire to check any places on that stretch of road that were open after ten last night. They have East's mugshot to show around.'

'Good work, well done. It has to be him, doesn't it – it all ties together: dumping one car, nicking another and driving to London. It's the obvious place for him to come to, he'd know a safe house or two. Be handy to find the car so Forensics could go over it.'

'What do you want done with the rest of the gang? They're all still locked up in Wales, sir?' Gheeta asked.

Palmer thought for a moment.

'Not going to get much from them, are we? Except Kershaw, he was important because of his brother-in-law. Get them released on unconditional bail, but have Kershaw brought here; I'd like a go at him. He must know who set this robbery up.'

'What about us, sir? Still need us?' Johnson asked, tentatively hoping for a 'yes'.

Palmer caught his drift and remembered the times when he was a young detective, and his excitement when seconded to a team on his first big murder case.

141

'Of course I still want you two on the team. You know the manor, the criminals on the manor and their habits. Get back down there and sniff around; lean on your contacts and see if anything gives. Then relieve the chaps on watch at Alexander's house and keep your eyes open. Unless you want to go back with DI Rayson and nick a couple of shoplifters?'

'No, sir,' they said in unison.

'I didn't think you would.'

He gave them a sly wink.

'Off you go then.'

Johnson and Simms left with a bounce in their walk. Palmer pointed after them. 'Good pair of coppers, that pair. Pity we haven't more like them.'

'I think you just added two more members to your fan club, guv,' Gheeta said.

'Really? I expect that's a big club,' he said, putting on a self-important smile.

Claire nodded.

'Yes. Counting me, the membership is up to three now.'

'Three?' said Palmer, feigning disappointment. He fixed accusing eyes on Gheeta. 'I would have expected *four*, at least. I hope your membership application is in the post sergeant?'

She held a hand in front of her and wobbled it like a small boat on a choppy sea.

'Not yet, guv. The jury's still out.'

****

Robert Kershaw arrived at the Yard early that afternoon, and Palmer took the five flights of stairs down to the basement interview rooms two at a time. When he got to the bottom his sciatica twinged and told him he should have taken the lift instead. He greeted George, the duty officer who sat at the end of the corridor signing suspects, prisoners and officers in and out.

'Afternoon, George. You okay?'

'I'm fine, Justin. You?'

'So far so good, George. Robert Kershaw is the chap I've come to see; my sergeant tells me he is all present and correct?'

'That he is, complete with his brief.'

'Anyone we know?'

'Duty solicitor,Freddy.'

'Oh good, we won't have any silly stalling then.'

143

Freddy Fredericks was a duty solicitor, one of a small band of local solicitors that would be happy to be assigned to each new prisoner being brought in for interrogation that did not have their own solicitor. Palmer and the other detectives liked Fredericks because he was one of the old school briefs who could see which way an interview was going, and not try to forestall the inevitable by advising the client to 'no comment' every question when the weight of evidence was so heavy a 'guilty' verdict was beyond doubt.

Palmer swapped perfunctory nods with Fredericks as he entered the interview room and took a seat opposite Fredericks and Kershaw. He leant and switched the interview recorder on.

'Interview room four, Tuesday 5th, 10 am. I am Detective Chief Superintendent Palmer, and present are Mr Fredericks the duty solicitor and Robert Kershaw, who I wish to question about several murders and the attempted robbery of the Royal Mint.'

He looked directly at Kershaw.

'Mr Kershaw, you are under caution. Do you know what that means?'

'Yes.'

144

'Good, then let me go over the events so far. You were unlawfully released from a prison van by George East and others to take part in a robbery at the Royal Mint in Wales. The other prisoners in the van were executed by a .22 handgun and their bodies set alight; they were Ali Kalhoud and Peter Shore. George Shore, the brother of Peter Shore, was also shot dead elsewhere, his body then put in the van and also set alight. The reason, as far as we know, for you being taken off that van was to take part in a robbery at the Royal Mint in Wales, where your brother in law Frederick Knoble worked as a security guard on the rear delivery gate. He was also later shot, but thankfully not fatally.

'The robbery was timed to take place on the very night that a substantial amount of gold bullion was being delivered. It is a reasonable assumption that you were the instigator of this robbery and a major player, without whom it would not take place; otherwise why take you off the prison van. So we have a total of three murders. A further Shore brother, Harry, was also shot dead earlier that day making four. All the shootings were carried out by the same gun associated with this job, and there – bang in the middle of this web of death –

is *you*. You may not have pulled the trigger, but it would seem you organised the shootings and bear the same responsibility in the eyes of the law as the shooter.'

He took a breath and hit Kershaw with his next shot.

'I will be charging you with being an accessory to the murders unless I hear anything from you to change that.'

Palmer sat back and waited. He knew he had overplayed Kershaw's part in the whole thing, but it was now up to Kershaw to extricate himself.

Kershaw sat for a moment, let out a deep breath, and then talked. From what Palmer had said to him he needed to talk, and he needed to talk a lot or he was in deep, deep trouble.

'It all went wrong, it wasn't supposed to end this way. I didn't know about the prison van; I didn't even know I was being sprung.'

Palmer shook his head and gave Kershaw a sarcastic smile..

'No, you were the key to the whole game. Without you and your brother-in-law, there was no robbery. You were so important that people were killed to get you onboard.'

'They were killed 'cause they wanted a part of it. They got wind of the job and threatened to blow it open if they weren't in.'

'So you had East kill them?'

Palmer knew if he kept up the pretence that he thought Kershaw was the main man he'd break and name names.

'I'm not the main man, I was only the link to Fred.'

'So Fred Knoble told you about the big shipment of gold going to the Mint?'

'Yes.'

'What was his cut going to be?'

'No, no, no, it wasn't like that. He wasn't in it at all. It was just something he said that started all this off. I was wanting to visit my sister socially – we'd had a row ages ago and I wanted to patch it up. But when I spoke to Fred on the phone about going down there, he said not to go on the first Friday of the month as he's always on gate duty because that's when bullion comes in; and especially not the first Friday in March as that's when the big load comes in.'

'So you saw an opportunity. And told who?'

'George East. I told George, thinking that sort of information was worth a few quid.'

147

'And was it?'

'Yes, he gave me a bung to keep my mouth shut about it and stay clean, and that was all. Never said I'd be involved, just told me to keep quiet. Then all this other shit happened.'

'Presumably because you didn't keep quiet about it?'

'Yes, we did a post office and got caught. I went down for a three stretch and shot my stupid mouth off to my cellmates.'

'Shore and Kalhoud.'

'Yes.'

'And Shore told his brothers, and they wanted in.'

'I didn't know that until after East pulled me off the van. I didn't know the Shores had done that.'

'Done what, asked to be in on the robbery?'

'Yeah, but the silly bastards threatened to grass it if they weren't in.'

Palmer paused for a few seconds.

'Bit of a silly move to pull on George East, wasn't it? He's not the kind of chap to threaten.'

'Bloody right he's not.'

'Nor is Frank Alexander.'

'I didn't know George had taken it to Alexander until after I was out of the van. I thought George was getting a team together on his own; I didn't know he'd taken the gig to Mr Alexander.'

Palmer noted the deference paid to *'Mr'* Alexander, reflected on the status of the man in the criminal fraternity and Kershaw's obvious fear of him.

'Okay, let's talk about what happened to the van and you afterwards. What happened when East pulled the van up?'

'I don't know, you can only see out sideways from the cubicles, not front or back. I didn't even know we'd been hijacked. Wasn't until we drew into the warehouse that we all realised something was up.'

'And what happened there?'

'East came in the back and let me out of the cage; he'd got the keys off the guard. I thought the others would be out too, but I didn't see them. I had a hood put over my head. I was told to keep quiet and hustled quickly out and taken away in a car. I didn't know what happened to them, I didn't see any shooting. It was only when I was taken to Mr Alexander's offices that I was told about that.'

'What were you told?'

149

'He said that because I'd mouthed off about the job in jail, Shore and his brothers had put the squeeze on and had been killed in case they blabbed about it to anybody else and wrecked the whole plan.'

'Bit over the top to kill them, wasn't it?'

'Lot of money involved. Fred had told me that sometimes twenty million in gold was delivered; a lot of money.'

'So I assume that you were kept at East's flat until the night of the robbery, in case you told anybody else?'

'No, he moved in with me at my place. It was only for a day.'

'In Clapham Road?'

'Yes

Palmer mentally kicked himself. He had surveillance on East's flat, on Alexander's offices and house and the snooker hall, hoping that East would go to one of them to lay low with Kershaw. He hadn't thought of Kershaw's flat. He ended the interview.

'Okay Mr Kershaw, that will do for now.'

'How's Fred, is he okay?'

'He's alive, he's in hospital, and probably looking forward to getting out and meeting his brother-in-law again. I'm sure he'll have a few things to say to you. Interview ends 10.20.'

He leant forward and flicked the recording button to off.

'I'll get a transcript of the recording to you ASAP, Mr Fredericks. In the meantime you can have as much time as you like with your client, but bail will be refused and he'll be kept in custody pending charges being brought against him.'

He nodded to them both and left the room.

****

'We didn't think of that.'

In the Team Room Palmer was still annoyed at his error.

'You don't kidnap somebody and take them back to their home, do you?'

Gheeta nodded in agreement.

'Not usually guv, no.'

'Get an armed response car to check it out; I can't think East would be there now, but just in case. And then get Frome to put a forensic team in and give it the once-over.'

Claire swung round in her chair.

'They've found the car he stole in Bristol, sir. Or what's left of it.'

She pointed up to one of the screens. A picture of a burnt-out car flashed up. Palmer peered forward at it.

'Where is it?'

'Under some railway arches in Acton.'

'Acton? Not giving away any clues is he, eh? He dumped it as soon as he got near the Mayor's Congestion Charge area, before it could get picked up by the NRCs. He's good. Better have Forensics take a look, but I can't imagine we will get anything relevant from it.'

Julie from the Media Centre entered. Palmer sighed an '*oh no what now?*' sigh.

'No, I haven't time for press conferences.'

Julie nodded.

'Yes, you have. Four o'clock in the media suite, update on the 'barbecue' killings.'

'The what?'

'The tabloids have christened the case 'the Barbecue Killings'.

'That is awful.'

He looked from Gheeta to Claire, who both had looks of horror on their faces.

'I know,' Julie agreed. 'That's why Bateman won't do it, and has shifted the conference onto your very capable broad shoulders again, Detective Chief Superintendent Palmer, sir.'

'You patronising sod.'

'I am, aren't I,' she laughed. 'But to be honest Justin, we thought you did a great job last time and have every confidence in you... sir.'

'Double patronising sod.'

'Okay, but jesting aside how do you want to handle it? The press boys know about the Royal Mint job, and the Knoble family have taken the king's shilling for their story so the press also know George East is in the frame as well and on the run.'

Palmer thought for moment.

'Okay, I'll concentrate on him then – the usual *'don't approach but call a copper'* line.'

'Good, I'll see you downstairs about ten to four; give me a bell if you need anything. By the way, where do you want your fan mail sent to?'

'Piss off.'

'I kid you not. We have a shoe-boxful since your last appearance on telly.'

Gheeta was stunned.

'Is that usual?'

Julie nodded.

'Yes, we always get a few; usually marriage proposals or death threats to the officer, but I have to admit, not usually this many. You're a star, Justin.'

'I don't want them,' Palmer said adamantly. 'Tell you what, readdress the death threats to Benji my next-door neighbour would you?'

'No, I'll have them all destroyed. That's the usual procedure.'

'Be interesting to read the marriage proposals,' Claire laughed.

'Some desperate women out there, eh?' Gheeta replied with a wink.

'Sad really.'

Claire shook her head and returned the wink. Palmer looked from one to the other.

'Have you two finished? We have a crime to solve, in case you had forgotten.'

He turned to Julie.

'Ten to four, I'll be there.'

****

The press conference went well; he had skirted round the awkward questions, kept his temper when some little oik from the *Guardian* kept on about why hadn't they got East already, and was it because he'd not enough men? Of course it was, but if he'd started on his views about police cuts he'd be in Bateman's office in the morning on a disciplinary charge. And he had to painstakingly explain to the man from the *Mail* who asked why the Firearms chaps hadn't shot East that if they had, under the current PCP rules they'd all be up on charges themselves; you can't just loose off at anybody these days, you have to give them warnings and dodge their bullets as you do so.

The rest of the afternoon had not brought any new leads on East, and Palmer was glad to get home and relax. He took Daisy for a walk round Dulwich Park, mainly to get away from the smoke from Benji's barbecue which was obviously still undergoing 'testing'; then he had a long relaxing soak in the bath and watched a Barcelona match on Sky, with a large glass of cider and a large bag of crisps. It was Mrs P.'s Women's Institute Committee Meeting night, so Daisy took advantage and lay on the sofa next to him, scrounging the odd crisp that made a dash for freedom 'twixt bag and mouth.

All the time his mind was turning over the case. Where was East? He was pretty sure he was still in the country; the red flags at Border Security are pretty reliable in picking out people. No, East was in London; he knew London, he had friends in London who would help him, especially Frank Alexander. He was a chip off the old block too. Palmer smiled as he recalled Frank's dad, George Alexander, and the look of surprise when a young DS Palmer and a team from the Organised Crime Squad led by 'Nipper' Read had pulled him out of bed at six in the morning, read him his rights, and arrested him for his part in the Knightsbridge Safe Deposit Robbery. Funny how life has a knack of repeating itself.

Oh well, what would tomorrow bring?

****

CHAPTER 21

Gail Alexander was not happy. They had not slept well after staying up until the small hours after East's second call and had cat-napped all day. They checked the TV news every hour, but no mention of East being arrested. Now the evening was closing in again as she poured another drink for herself and one for Frank from a decanter on an antique rosewood desk, and they both stood looking out of the large French windows onto the long back garden and the golf course beyond as they sipped. No chance of that view changing; that golf course would never be developed for housing, certainly not while Frank was on the committee.

It was an expensive house on the fringes of Blackheath, set well away from the road and prying eyes with large gardens that a gardener took care of. They entertained, and were entertained; their humble background of petty crime in south London, that had grown to major crime and had financed, and still financed, their expensive life style was kept well under wraps. Frank was a successful city businessman – that was the mantra played out whenever anybody asked; and as long as the Alexanders kept donating well to local causes, nobody could be bothered to look any further.

'What if he comes here?'

'He won't, I told him to stay away. He'll know we are being watched, so he won't come here.'

'Are you sure you are in the clear on this?'

'Yes. George got the gun, *he* rented it; the lot he got it from don't know me.'

'Your big *signature* job has turned out to be a real failure hasn't it, eh?'

'Yep. Freddy Doorman told me to take care when that Palmer copper got involved. Said he was good.'

'Freddy was right. What are you going to do about George?'

'With a bit of luck they nabbed him at the snooker hall.'

He finished his drink and poured himself another one.

'He's got nothing on me, nothing to tie me in with this.'

'Christ, Frank, don't be a fool. He's been with you for years, and knows all about your businesses.'

'All legit, nothing to hide now. Books and accounts up-to-date.'

'Except the offshore ones.'

'Too well-hidden, they couldn't find those.'

'I hope you're right, 'cause East will take a deal if it means a softer charge. You know he will.'

The front doorbell rang. Frank turned and placed his drink on the table.

'I bet that's the law. If they haven't a search warrant they're not coming in.'

Gail snapped at him.

'Don't be stupid! Remember, we don't know anything about this – nothing. You let them in, and if they say anything about last night act surprised. Use your head, Frank.'

He nodded and left the lounge. In the hall he flicked on the porch light before opening the door. Nobody was there. He stepped out and looked around; nobody. His mind raced. It must be East. What's he playing at? What is his game?

He stepped back inside and closed the door, clicking down the security lock. Down the hall he went into the kitchen and pulled open the cutlery drawer set in the side of an old oak dining table. The drawer pulled right out, it was shorter than its housing. Frank reached inside to the back and pulled out a Glock 26 pistol, the magazine already loaded.

He put the drawer back, held the gun down by his side, and made his way back to the lounge.

Gail was seated in an armchair, with George East stood behind her holding his gun to her head. Frank noted one of the French doors was slightly open, showing where East had entered from.

'Don't even raise the gun Frank, or she's dead. Throw it onto the sofa.'

He did as he was told.

'What are you doing, George? You need to get away, what's all this about?'

'It's about you grassing me, Frank.'

'Are you kidding?'

'Only one person knew I was going to the snooker hall, Frank: *you*. You told me to go there. So how comes the police were there soon after, Frank? Eh? Explain that. You think I'm so stupid as to fall for that old trick? You pulled that one on Harry Belton, remember that do you? After we did the Graff jewellery shop; put a bit of the loot in a safe house in Eltham and told Harry to lay low there, and then sent the law round. He's still doing his time on that. I'm not doing time on this one, Frank, oh no. This is too big. If they get me on this I'm up on first degree, four times. They'll throw the key away, and I'm not about to let them do that.'

'What are you going to do.'

'It's not what I'm going to do, Frank. It's what *you* are going to do.'

'Me?'

'Yes, you. And I'll tell you what you are going to do. You are going to go to your office and open the safe and bring back the two hundred grand you keep inside it. I am going to have that money Frank, and then you will never see me again. If you think that instead of going to the office you might go and tell the police I'm here, think again Frank; if I so much as suspect they are coming for me, Gail will die. I'm on the sheet for four murders Frank, so one more won't make a difference. Understand? One sniff of a copper, and bang-bang – bye-bye Gail. There's an Audi squad car outside, fifty yards down the road with two plainclothes blokes in it. If anymore arrive when you're gone, bang-bang.'

'Do it, Frank,' Gail said, her voice faltering. 'We can make the money back. Do as he says.'

Frank feigned reticence while his mind slipped into overdrive.

'Okay, but then you go, George. You go, and you stay gone.'

East nodded.

'That's the deal. And you come back from the office alone; no funny business.'

Frank pulled his motor slowly out of his drive onto the main road; he noted the plain squad car parked further down and passed it without looking. It drew out fifty metres behind and slotted into the following traffic.

In the Team Room Gheeta spoke to Johnson and Simms in the tail car on the comms as Palmer listened and watched the moving light on the screen.

'Is he alone, two-seven?'

'Yes, looks like it,' Simms replied. 'Unless he's got anybody hidden on the floor.'

Palmer leant towards the mic.

'Two-seven, this is Palmer. Take care and keep with him. If East managed to get into the house without us knowing, Alexander could well be trying to smuggle him out somewhere. Just remember East has a gun, and has used it.'

'Will do, sir.'

Gheeta took over as Palmer stood back.

'We have eyes on you, two-seven. Looks like he's heading into town.'

Frank kept an eye on the following car. No need to try and lose it, he was in the clear; to all intents and purposes he was just going about his own business. The traffic was not thick at that time of night and soon he was parked in his office space at the Shard underground car park and making his way up to reception.

He signed in with the night duty staff, passed a few comments about the weather and took the lift to his offices. From the front office's one-way glass windows he could see the squad car waiting on the road below.

'I won't be long, chaps.'

He opened the safe and looked at the bundles of banknotes, his '*sprint*' money: money kept ready in case things came tumbling down to such a degree that he had get out quick. He should never have let East know it was there. In all their years together he had never really trusted him, but in the business Frank had been in and to some extent was still in you needed a minder with a nasty reputation, and East certainly had that.

He put the money into a small attaché case and then, opening the base drawer of the safe, removed a large manila envelope of papers. He was finished; job done.

He locked the office and took the lift to the ground floor, signed out, bid the security staff a good night, and took the stairs down to the car park.

As he waited for the car park barrier to raise and let him out, he could see the squad car.

'This way gentlemen,' he muttered as the barrier rose and he drove out.

****

'Two-seven. He's leaving and heading south towards the Elephant and Castle. He has a small briefcase and some papers with him now.'

'Didn't he have them when he went in to the building?' Gheeta asked, puzzled.

'No.'

Palmer and Gheeta exchanged glances.

'What's he up to?'

Palmer took a chair as Claire came into the room carrying coffees.

'What's who up to? I had to go up to the machine on the fifth floor for these,' she said, putting the coffees down. 'Our machine is broken again.'

'Good, I'm sure they get a better coffee up there than the dishwater we have to put up with.'

'It's what is Frank Alexander up to,' Gheeta answered in reply to Claire's question. 'He's been into his office and got a case and some papers, and now he's heading South.'

She pointed to the flashing LED on the screen.

'That's our car tailing him.'

Claire sat and sipped her coffee.

'Perhaps he's got some money and passports and is doing a runner.'

Palmer sipped his coffee.

'I knew it! I bloody well knew it!'

He took another sip. Gheeta didn't understand.

'Knew what, guv? That he's doing a runner?'

'No, I bloody well knew that Bateman and his top brass cronies on the fifth floor would have a decent blend of coffee in their damn machine. It actually tastes like coffee, not dishwater like ours does. Crafty buggers.'

He calmed down and put the cup down.

'No, Alexander isn't doing a runner. Why would he? We haven't got anything on him to connect him to either the failed robbery or any of the murders. But he's up to something.'

The comms crackled.

'Two-seven. He's turned down the Old Kent Road.'

Palmer and Gheeta looked at each other and spoke in unison.

'Freddy Doorman.'

****

'Well, well, well, Mr Alexander, what brings you out at this time of night? It's nearly closing time.'

Freddy Doorman rose from his table at the Walmer Castle, put down the evening paper he had been reading, motioned his two minders away and shook Frank's hand. The pair of them sat down.

'Not just a social visit I'm sure, not this late.'

'Business, Freddy; social and business never mix, you know that. I think I may have a problem that you can help me with.'

'If I can I will, Frank. You know that.'

'I take it you've been watching the antics of George on the news?'

'Can't miss it, can you? Four dead and he's on the run; even got Palmer doing the press conferences. They want him badly don't they, Frank. Would have been a master hit if that job had come off though, a master hit.'

'Yes, would have been. But it wasn't, and it's all got a bit silly, Freddy.'

'So what can I do for you then?'

'Well, George has flipped his lid, and at this present time he has Gail as a hostage.'

Doorman raised his eyebrows.

'You are joking?'

'No, not joking. He's waiting for me to bring him enough cash to get a quick flight out of the country.'

'Tell me where he is Frank, and I'll have a few of my people take care of it and bring Gail back here.'

Frank held up his hands.

'No, no, thanks for the offer but that is not what I want. I'm going to give him the cash,

Freddy, and if he keeps his word he'll just go. Probably with Gail.'

'With Gail?'

'They've had a thing going for ages. Wouldn't surprise me if she goes with him. She's got her own Swiss bank account and her name's on the deeds to the Tenerife villa, and most of the business is in her name.

'You trust him to keep his word and just go?'

'Ah, now that's where you might come in. No, I don't trust him; or her. Listen Freddy, if anything goes wrong and I somehow meet my end...'

'Now I know you are joking...' Doorman interrupted. 'Aren't you?'

'No Freddy, I'm not. I'm deadly serious. I've known East for an awful long time, and I know how violent he can be. I'm going to give him a good wedge to get him out of the country and set himself up abroad somewhere. But if he thinks I'm going to cough up anymore, he's wrong.'

He looked round to make sure they were out of earshot to anybody else and leant forward close to Doorman's face. He spoke softly for a minute or two before leaning back.

'So that's the deal, Freddy. Will you take care of it?'

Doorman was very serious.

'Frank, should it be necessary, it will be a pleasure.'

Frank hoisted the manila envelope onto the table and pushed it across to Doorman.

'That's payment in advance, Freddy. Non-returnable. If everything works out and the deal's off, it's still yours.'

Doorman looked inside the packet.

'Bearer Bonds.'

'Two hundred grand's worth, Freddy. Cashable anywhere in the world, with no questions asked.'

'Frank, this is not necessary. I go back a long way with your family, you know how close me and your dad were in the bad old days.'

He laughed.

'I'd do it for his memory, Frank. I don't want paying.'

He pushed the envelope back across the table. Frank pushed it back again.

'I need you take it, Freddy. You know the way it works in our line of business; if I pay for something and shake on it, we have a deal, signed and sealed; if I don't pay it's not a deal, it's a favour. I only work in deals, Freddy. Do we have a deal?'

He held out a hand. Freddy Doorman looked Frank straight in the eyes for a moment, and then took his hand and shook it.

'We have a deal, Frank. We have a deal.'

'Thank you, Freddy.'

****

'Two-seven. He's on the move again but no package; whatever it was he's left it at the pub.'

Palmer watched the indicator light shift along the map.

'Where's he off to now then? With a bit of luck it's to meet East.'

A new voice came over the comms.

'Three-one to Palmer.'

Palmer looked at Claire expectantly and mouthed the question: *'three-one?'*.

'They slotted in to two- seven's place at the Alexander house sir,' she advised him.

Palmer nodded.

'Go ahead, three-one,' Gheeta said.

'Three-one, we have a visitor at the house.'

'Can you see who it is, three-one?'

'No, he or she has kept close to the hedge and has spoken into the gate intercom. The gates opened and the person has entered, then the gate closed again.'

'Okay three-one, remain where you are.'

Gheeta turned to Palmer.

'East?'

'Got to be, hasn't it? He can't just disappear into thin air, and Alexander probably knows the right people to get him out of the country, so he needs to make contact. Get an armed task force to quietly attend; no fuss, just to wait out of sight until we can get more information.'

'How are we going to get that, guv?'

'That house backs onto a golf course.'

He stood and started to put his coat on.

'Bring one of your listening things Sergeant, and we'll get as close as we can round the back and see if we can pick up a conversation.'

'Listening thing, guv? It is a very precise piece of kit called an ADA – an Audio Directional Amplifier.'

She rummaged round in a side cupboard and hoisted one out. Palmer straightened his trilby.

'I haven't been on a golf course for ages.'

'I didn't know you played golf, guv?'

'I don't.'

Claire and Gheeta exchanged glances. There was no answer to that.

Frank Alexander watched his double security gates close slowly behind him as he drove back into his drive; his tail had pulled in a hundred metres up the road. He smiled to himself. If he needed the police, they wouldn't take long to arrive.

He parked up and went back into the house, the briefcase of money held firmly by his side. He intended to get rid of East as soon as he could.

In the lounge, East stood by the French doors. Gail was still seated on the sofa, and surprise surprise… Kershaw was sitting next to her.

'We have a visitor.'

East used his gun's barrel as a pointer. Alexander nodded.

'So I see. What brings you here? I thought they were holding you?'

'I got bailed. Palmer couldn't make any charges stick other than 'intent to rob', could he? So I got bailed.'

'So you led them here, then.'

'Who?'

'The police! You don't think for one moment they are not following you, do you? Every copper in London is looking for George, and you've just led them straight to him.'

'I didn't know he'd be here, did I?'

'So what do you want then? Why come here?'

'Palmer wants to know all about the job. He knows I must be in it from the beginning 'cause of Fred working at the Mint; so he knows I can, as he put it, *be of great help*.''

'You mean grass on us.'

'*Be of great help*, he said.'

'In exchange for what?'

'No charges brought against me.'

Frank laughed.

'He's having a game with you, Kershaw. He couldn't do that – even *Palmer*

173

couldn't do that. You've been nicked, you're on file, charges will be brought. So what's he really offered you?'

'Said he'd give me a good reference to the court and could probably reduce my sentence. Might even get away with a non-custodial.'

'If you were to *be of great help*, eh?'

'Yes.'

'And are you going to *be of great help*, Kershaw?'

'Depends, doesn't it.'

'On what?'

'Well, I thought you might be very grateful if I turned down his offer.'

'How grateful would that be then?'

'Fifty grand grateful.'

East shook his head in disbelief.

'I know a cheaper way.'

And he walked over to Kershaw and shot him in the head.

'Problem solved.'

Frank Alexander could hardly believe what he had witnessed. Kershaw's body slipped sideways across Gail's lap, the blood dripping down her leg as she stifled a scream with her hands and turned white. Frank stepped forward and pulled it off her onto the floor.

'You stupid fuck! What was that about? Now we have a body to get rid of!'

'Two bodies actually,' said East, and raising the gun again he shot Frank Alexander in the heart. He crumpled to the floor, stone dead before he hit it.

East picked up the briefcase. Gail stayed rooted to the sofa for a few seconds before finding her voice. She spoke slowly.

'What have you done, George?'

'What I planned to do,' he said with a smile. 'I planned to kill Frank; had to. Once we took the money and scarpered, he'd have had a contract out on us. There's no way he would just sit and let us get away with it, would he.'

'But why kill Kershaw?'

'He'd be a witness, wouldn't he? Anyway, him coming here has worked out for the good.'

'Good how?'

'They had a row. Kershaw shot Frank and put the gun down to get the money, Frank managed to get to it and shot Kershaw, and then died himself.'

He wiped the gun on the curtains and then knelt beside Frank Alexander's body and pressed it into his dead hand, curling a finger round the trigger.

'There we are, Frank's prints on the gun. Sorted.'

'Not quite, George.'

He turned to find Gail had the Glock that Frank had thrown onto the sofa earlier, and it was pointing at his head.

'What are you doing, you stupid cow? Put it down.'

'Do you really think I'd give all this up for a life on the run with you, George? You were fun while it lasted, but that was all it was ever going to be, George. Sorry.'

The shot was loud, no silencer; it went straight through George East's head, leaving a nasty splayed-out exit hole at the back which leaked blood onto the carpet where he fell. Gail quickly took the gun in Frank Alexander's hand and wiped it before pressing it into East's hand, then she wiped the Glock and pressed it into Frank Alexander's hand.

She picked up the briefcase of money and took a large picture down off the wall which revealed a wall safe. She entered the combination, opened it, put the money from the case inside, closed it, replaced the picture, and put the now empty briefcase in a cupboard. She stood and looked around the room; perfect.

She walked over to the side table and pressed a panic button hidden beneath its top. Then she ripped her top, dishevelled her hair and scratched her own face. That hurt. Then she ran to the front door, opened it, and ran screaming down the drive.

****

Palmer got the call on the radio from Johnson as they were on their way to the golf course.

'Gail Alexander said what?' he asked, hardly believing what he'd heard.

Johnson repeated it.

'She came running and screaming down the drive, and she says there are three dead in the house, sir: East, Kershaw, and her husband. She's very shook up. Medics are on their way.'

'Okay, we will give Frome a call and get his SOCA crew down there. You and Simms better seal the area.'

'Will do, sir.'

Palmer told the driver to make for the house, not the golf course, and gave Gheeta a wide-eyed look and a shrug that said: 'What the hell is going on?'

Gheeta took a long breath.

'That's six dead now, guv.'

'That'll please Bateman.'

****

DI Rayson met them as their car pulled up on the drive in front of Alexander's house.

'Blimey, you got here quick,' said Palmer as he got out, trying hard not to wince at the sciatic pain that stabbed his thigh.

'We got a call from Alexander's security alarm company. Apparently somebody pressed one of the panic buttons in the house; that alerts the alarm people and they phoned it through to us. I'd already got this address flagged up as '*of interest*' in our despatch room, so they gave me a call. Looks like a right mess in there. Gail Alexander has been given a sedative and taken to the station to give a statement.'

Palmer nodded.

'She the only witness?'

'Yes, in a bit of a state but she came up through the criminal world with Frank, so from what I remember of interviewing her in the distant past she's quite a tough one. Do you want to see her? She won't say a word until her solicitor arrives, I can tell you that. Frank trained her well.'

'No, I don't think so; not yet anyway. Get a copy of her statement through to us if you would.'

'Yes, of course.'

He nodded towards the house.

'I understand Frome is on his way with a SOCA team, so we've not disturbed anything. Want to take a look?'

'Of course.'

Rayson went to the open boot of a patrol car and took out two pairs of shoe covers.

'Here you are, put these on and then feel free. Oh, and by the way, can I have my two officers back now? I have more than enough on my plate for the low number of chaps I've got without missing some.'

Palmer laughed.

'I thought you'd be having a quiet time, seeing as we had most of the faces from your patch banged up in Wales.'

Rayson smiled.

'Yes, but you let the bastards out again. Now they'll want to make up for lost earnings, and you've two of my best men with you.'

'Okay,' said Palmer, 'Let me have them for this evening, and then I'll sign them back to you tomorrow. I must say though, they're a good pair of coppers, did well for me; a real compliment to your team. I think they deserve a few days off.'

'No way,' Rayson said, looking aghast at the suggestion. 'I'll leave you the uniform boys tonight to secure the premises. Keep me up-to-date, won't you.'

'Of course.'

Rayson gave a perfunctory nod to both Palmer and Singh, got in his car and was driven off.

They mounted the steps to the Alexanders' door and flashed their cards at the uniform officer barring their way. Inside they found Johnson and Simms at the door to the lounge, also with overshoes on.

'Bit like a murder mystery in there, sir,' said Simms. 'Three bodies, two guns, and the sole witness too distraught to talk.'

Palmer walked carefully into the room, followed by Singh and the officers. He looked at the scene.

'Well, at least it will save the taxpayer a great deal of money not having to keep this lot banged up for life.'

That wasn't the statement Johnson and Simms had expected. They looked at Singh, who rolled her eyes and shrugged; she had realised long ago that Palmer often said what the public felt, and what senior officers were not supposed to say.

Palmer slowly walked round the room, taking in the scene.

'Mrs Alexander's statement is going to make interesting reading.'

'Do you want her brought to the Yard tomorrow for an interview, sir? She should have her brief by then,' Gheeta asked.

'No, I don't think so; anyway, not until Mr Frome and his SOCA team have had a good look at this lot. Mind you, if her fingerprints are on both the guns she'll have a bit of explaining to do. But I'll bet they aren't.'

'She was a bit confused when she came down the drive, sir,' Johnson explained. 'But the gist of what she said was that East shot Kershaw, and then Alexander and East shot each other.'

'Could well have happened that way, we'll see. Right then, not a lot we can do

181

here. Rayson has insisted you go back tomorrow, so if you'll hang on here for Mr Frome and turn the crime scene over to him, that should see you two finished. He will arrange for Pathology to remove the bodies.'

You could almost hear their faces drop. Palmer shook their hands.

'My Serial Murder Squad is a small unit, lads; just myself, Detective Sergeant Singh here, and Claire. So we have a list of tried and tested detectives from other units that we call on when we need more boots on the ground, as was the case with this little caper. You two are now on that list, gentlemen. So, in the words of that awful Vera Lynn song... we'll meet again.'

They turned and left the room.

'Vera Lynn, guv? That's a new one.'

'Didn't I ever tell you about the time I pushed her off a chair?'

'You what?'

She looked at him, wide-eyed.

'I was eight years-old. I had queued for an hour at the annual Boys and Girls Exhibition at Olympia to get Tom Finney's autograph, and just when I was next in the line he buggered off and Vera Lynn took his place.'

'So you pushed her off her chair?'

'Well not intentionally, no. But her daughter snatched my autograph book and put in front of her to sign, and I tried to snatch it back. She held on and I held on, but she was stronger and I let go, and she toppled backwards off her chair.'

'Oh my God!' Gheeta laughed.

'Wasn't funny at the time; I was hauled into the security office and they phoned my dad to come and collect me.'

'I bet he was pleased,' she said sarcastically.

'Ex-Eighth Army, The Desert Rats; Vera had been out to the desert to entertain them in the war, so he wasn't pleased, no. Must have slapped me round the head twenty times on the way home. Mum was more sympathetic though when I explained about the autograph book.'

'Was she?'

'yes, she only slapped me round the head ten times.'

****

CHAPTER 22

There was nothing urgent to do with the case; it felt like it had wound itself up on its own, so Palmer decided he and Gheeta would have the next morning off to relax for a few hours and recharge the batteries. Reg Frome's initial Forensic Report and the Pathology Report wouldn't be ready until the afternoon, so the only business would be to update AC Bateman. Get it out of the way first was Palmer's thoughts as he trudged up to the fifth floor that afternoon. He'd spent the morning at home, not relaxed recharging his batteries but writing out a brief update report on the activities of the previous day; Bateman was a stickler for reports and paperwork and Palmer found it less hassle to just give him something to read, however light and incomplete; otherwise there would be memos flying down from above asking for updates.

The rest of the morning had been spent taking Daisy round Dulwich Park for a walk, and avoiding Benji who was pottering about in his garden with the barbecue and sending puffs of smoke up into the air like a Red Indian message.

He got to the office early in the afternoon and checked in with Claire to see if there was any statement from Gail Alexander posted on file as yet. There wasn't.

****

'Well, that was a bit of a surprise ending.'

Bateman put down the report on his desk and sat back in his chair.

'I thought it tidied everything up nicely, sir,' said Palmer, raising his eyebrows questionably.

'Certainly does that.'

'You'll be able to give the press a happy ending, sir.'

'Happy?'

'Well, no members of the public were injured, except poor old Fred Knoble; no imminent gang wars on London's streets; and DCS Palmer triumphs again. Don't forget to tell them that last bit, sir.'

He gave Bateman a big smile, which was returned.

'Yes, well I'll go along with the no public injured and no imminent gang wars, but I think I'll leave out the bit about DCS Palmer triumphs again. I understand your fan mail is beginning to clog up our post box as it is.'

'On a serious note sir, I think we ought to hang fire on any press statement until I get the witness statement from Gail Alexander, just to be on the safe side. One thing has been bothering me about the shootings.'

'Go on?'

'Why wasn't she shot? If East killed Frank and had made off, I'm sure she'd put out a big money contract on him; so why didn't he shoot her too?

'Frank Alexander shot him before he could?'

'Maybe, but the sequence of the shots is just bugging me.'

Bateman knew that if something was bugging Palmer, there would be a reason; he may not have liked Palmer that much as a person and would have dearly loved to combine the Serial Murder Squad with Organised Crime, but when it came to doing the job Palmer was top man. If he wasn't happy about something, his intuitions had come up tops so many times in the past that it was best to let him run with it.

'Okay,' Bateman nodded. 'Let me know when you are happy to close it.'

He stood up, which was the signal that the interview was over. Palmer stood and ferreted around in his pocket, bringing out a pound coin.

'You haven't any change for a pound sir, have you?'

'Change for a pound? Whatever for?'

'I want to take a couple of coffees down to Sergeant Singh and Claire; you get a better blend up here in your machine than we do downstairs. I've got one fifty pence, need two more.'

Bateman checked his change and did the swap. At the machine Palmer fed the first two coins in – milk no sugar for Gheeta, milk with sugar for Claire – and put their coffees on a window sill. He fed the last fifty pence coin in for his cup – black no milk no sugar – and watched as the inviting dark liquid streamed down Trouble was, the cup that should have preceded it didn't.

****

When he got back to the Team Room he gave Gheeta and Claire their coffees, sneaked a fifty pence piece from the drawer in his office and joined them with a cup of dishwater from the machine on their floor. Gheeta set a printer buzzing away.

'Gail Alexander's witness statement is through, sir; pretty straightforward. Seems East sneaked in from the golf course where he'd been hiding in a green keeper's hut all day. An argument started because Kershaw, who must have been the chap our guys saw go in the front, wanted money, or he'd tell the police Alexander was involved in the robbery. She says he wasn't and it was all East's doing, and the first she and her husband knew about it was when it was on the news. East lost his temper with Kershaw and shot him, and when Alexander refused to give East money to get him out of the country, he accused him of *grassing* – her word not mine – and shot him too; then he was about to do the same to Gail when Frank, who was injured down on the floor, pulled a gun and shot him. Bang, bang, bang: three corpses.'

She pulled a copy off the printer and handed it to Palmer. He read it in silence for a while.

'Total rubbish. We know Frank Alexander knew what was happening 'cause he was at the snooker club; and what was he doing going to his office earlier that evening and then onto Freddy Doorman's? She must know what he was doing; she's been coached through this. Who is her brief?'

Claire looked at the screen.

'Bird's Solicitors, Wandsworth.'

'Oh right, the top criminal defence solicitor's firm. Yes, she's been coached through this alright.

'Do you want to bring her in for a chat now then, guv?' asked Gheeta.

'No, I don't think so; not yet, anyway – she'd just stick to this story. We can't disprove it, and I can't see her shooting anybody; no reason to. She's living the good life; if anybody fell into a barrel of pooh and came up smelling of roses, Gail Alexander did. Unless the fingerprints tell a different story, she's just a witness.'

They didn't. The fingerprints forensics found confirmed Gail Alexander's story of who shot whom with which gun.

The coroner held inquests, and as all three deceased were murdered by 'person or persons known', the inquests were standard procedure and closed. The bodies were released to the families and Bateman decided to slip the case into 'non-priority' status, with a view to closing it when all the reports were filed and signed off. Palmer wasn't too happy at that, but all he had was a hunch, a feeling that something was not right; and you can't keep a case open on a hunch.

Robert Kershaw's funeral was quite well-attended by the South London petty criminal element, although the Knoble family didn't show. George East's was very quiet with few mourners, but Frank Alexander's was the full menu: horse-drawn glass carriage carpeted in white bloom wreaths, second carriage with Gail and family members, then twenty-two stretch limos full of the rich and powerful of the UK crime scene, from London, Manchester, Liverpool and Glasgow, including Freddy Doorman and his minders, plus a few of the past 'names' from the Richardsons' gang and others who were still alive. They recounted past demeanours as they packed the church alongside the new kids on the block, who were paying their false respects to Gail while working out which parts of Frank's empire they could now muscle in on with East out of the way.

Taking full advantage of the occasion, the Met's Organised Crime Division had eight 'snappers' covering the funeral, sending hundreds of digital pictures of known and unknown faces back to be run through the

Automatic Facial Recognition database, analysed and filed on hard disks. They also had two video operators live-streaming back to the office from good vantage points they had taken up long before the hearse and mourners arrived.

Palmer had also taken advantage of Alexander's funeral being on a Saturday to avoid Benji's barbecue. He sat in the Organised Crime team room with Gheeta and some of the OC officers, watching the big screen as the video streams from the funeral came in.

He had asked Gheeta to come along, although it was a Saturday and the case was closed, as he saw it as an opportunity to introduce her to some of the Organised Crime Division detectives, as he was sure that as soon as Bateman managed to retire him the Serial Murder Squad would be amalgamated with OCD to cut costs.

'If we could go in now and put this lot behind bars for a few years, we'd solve ninety per cent of UK crime in one go,' said an OCD Superintendent.

Palmer nudged Gheeta and pointed at the screen.

'There's Freddy Doorman. Good heavens, he's with Chris Lambrianou! I thought he was dead.'

'Who, guv?' asked Gheeta.

'Chris Lambrianou, one of the Lambrianou brothers; part of the Krays' firm. That's Eddie Richardson, too – he must be pushing ninety now, and he's got half his old firm with him. Oh, here come the big boys.'

He pointed out some figures.

'That's the Adams family – thought they were all inside, must be on day release. There's two of the Araf brothers, and, if my eyes don't deceive me, Mr Noye and Mr Norris in deep conversation with David Hunt and Michael Seed. Seed is rumoured to be the Hatton Garden robber they called 'Basil'.

He sat back in his chair and let out a long breath.

'Well, well, well, I had no idea Alexander was riding in such exalted company.'

The OCD Superintendent laughed.

'Maybe he wasn't. These top guys use a funeral as a legitimate cover to meet and do business. Probably be a few million quid's worth of cocaine deals done in the back pews of that church today.'

****

CHAPTER 23

All was not well; all was definitely not well. As Palmer arrived home he couldn't turn and park in his front drive because it was blocked... by a fire engine.

He followed the hose from the fire engine up his front garden, along the side path of the house and into the back garden where the firemen were clearing up what was left of two burnt fencing panels and some charred remnants of one of Mrs P.'s prized yellow buddleia shrubs.

Through the burnt-out gap he could see a small crowd of what must have been barbecue guests standing well back on Benji's lawn – or what was left of it – their plates and wine glasses discarded beside them. Benji and Mrs P. stood in front of them, watching the firemen work; both had blackened faces, and Harry and Meghan on Benji's tee-shirt had blackened faces too from where he had wiped his hands.

Palmer stood on his side of the gap and looked across to them.

'How was the barbecue?' he asked with a sarcastic lilt to his voice.

'It melted and fell onto the fence,' came a near-tearful reply from Benji.

'It what?'

One of the firemen looked over to Palmer.

'Chinese, cheap metal – low melt point. Should be banned.'

'Bit late now.'

Mrs P. moved nearer.

'Those damn rocks got too hot; it was supposed to turn itself down, but the thermostat must have failed. They just exploded and the whole lot sort of collapsed in a molten heap against our fence, and the lot went up like a bonfire.'

'Anybody hurt?' Palmer thought he had better ask.

'No.'

'Well, I did say you can't have a barbecue without charcoal. Hot rocks indeed.'

He moved a smouldering piece of fence with his foot.

'There is a good side to all this.'

'There is?' Benji said, brightening up.

'Yes, you've got plenty of charcoal for next time.'

****

CHAPTER 24

After the funerals the press got bored and moved onto other things. Gheeta and Claire put the final case reports together for Palmer to sign off, and Bateman officially closed it after receiving them; after a fortnight Palmer had to admit he hadn't anything concrete that could be used as a reason to keep the case active.

He still had that unfinished business feeling, probably because it was unusual to close a case without having some villain being put away for a number of years; and as his cases involved serial murders it was usually a fair number of years. But not this time; that was a strange feeling.

The *eureka* moment came as he shuffled once more through the logistics of the Alexander house killings. Everything was fine and dandy in the SOCA and Pathology reports, except for one thing. It was in the Pathology report on East. He died from a single shot to the temple with an exit wound at the back of the head; but the diagram of the bullet's route showed the exit wound below that of the entry wound on the temple. Palmer hurriedly checked the photos of East from the Path Lab. Sure

195

enough, the exit wound was below the entry wound, a good fifteen centimetres below.

Palmer sat back in his chair and pushed it up on its back legs against the wall where it slotted into a large groove he had made over the years. He ran through Gail Alexander's statement.

'East was about to shoot me when Frank, who was injured and dying on the floor, pulled a gun out and managed to shoot him...'

Palmers brain went into overdrive.

How can a bullet, fired from the floor upwards into the temple of a man standing up, do a U-turn and exit at a lower place than it entered?

It couldn't. Gail Alexander was lying.

****

Bateman took a little convincing to reopen the case and would have to get permissions from above his pay grade to do so, but the Pathology Report clinched it, and he knew that Palmer would be like a dog with a bone until he was satisfied that Gail Alexander was either a killer or had made a mistake in her statement and needed to rectify it. As there was no great urgency, no further lives at risk, it took a further fortnight for the powers that be to permit the case to go live again, and for Palmer to set up an interview with Gail Alexander under caution.

****

The Alexander house was empty, a For Sale sign wired to the gates. The estate agent quoted *'data protection'* when refusing to give Palmer Gail Alexander's new place of abode, and Palmer quoted *'obstructing the police in their line of duty and a night in a cell'*, which loosened the agent's tongue. Gail had put everything into the hands of her solicitors, the sale of the business's and the house.

The solicitors were more cooperative and quite agreeable to Gail being interviewed personally; they would have to ask her, of course, and the trouble was, she had moved lock stock and barrel to the Alexander house on Tenerife. It was in her name, so why shouldn't she try and start a new life out there?

It only took a couple of days for the solicitors to come back with an answer: yes, she was quite happy to be interviewed out there.

It took considerably longer for Palmer to get permission – firstly from 'upstairs' to take a trip to the Canaries, and secondly from the local police on the island who are split into three separate forces, with each one having to okay the trip, and all wanting to know the reason for the interview as it had taken a long time to rid the Canaries of the bad name it had for being a safe haven for gangsters on the run.

Three weeks later, all was in place. Mrs P. packed a tube of sun cream factor five in Palmer's overnight bag, although he kept telling her he would be in and out in a day and would not be lounging on a beach.

'You'll still be in the hot sun, not worth taking the risk. Skin cancer can kill.'

'So can dodgy barbecues.'

****

CHAPTER 25

The day was hot, the sun was blazing down on the Island of Tenerife, and Gail Alexander was relaxing beside the pool at her luxury villa.

It had been a busy three months since Frank's death. Lawyers had managed to sell most of the businesses – the legal ones, that is – and she had transferred money from the offshore accounts into just one in her name in Panama. She had stood back from any of his non-legal enterprises and cut them dead, letting others fight for the spoils; she had enough to secure a very wealthy future for herself. All in all, it had worked out very well for her, and she was still young enough and had the looks to maybe snare another husband from the wealthy ex-pat community on the island; some elderly gent with loads of money and a short life expectancy would fit the bill.

The buzzer from the security gates at the road sounded. A quick look at the screen showed a taxi waiting. Was Palmer early? His flight wasn't due in for another two hours. He must have got an earlier one. She pushed the button to open the gates and let it through to the marble steps that led up to the front entrance doors. She was due to have an evening meal at the top Italian restaurant in town later, with two wealthy widows from the ex-pat club who had taken her under their wing, thinking she was just a young widow in mourning; so Palmer being early would suit her just fine. She had spent the morning going over her statement about the shootings and was confident there was nothing that could be challenged if she stuck to it. The solicitor had told her not to worry, and that it was just a formality to close the case once and for all.

Opening the front door she was very surprised to see Freddy Doorman standing there, looking every part the local ex-pat in a light beige cotton suit, Rayban sunglasses and sandals.

'Freddy! What…?'

'Hello, Gail. Just a quick visit. I've got a message from Frank that I promised him I'd give you.'

'A message from Frank? He's dead!'

'Yes, he is – otherwise I wouldn't have to give you the message. Frank said to tell you 'goodbye.''

The hand Freddy drew from behind his back held a pistol with which he shot Gail in

200

the temple. She crumpled to the ground, and he made sure that she stayed there with one more shot to the head. Then, turning, he looked skywards and smiled.

'We had a deal, Frank; and Freddy Doorman always makes good on his deals.'

He walked down the steps, got into the taxi, and his minder drove it out of the villa's grounds towards the airport. On the floor in the back lay a local taxi driver, blood oozing from the bullet hole in his temple.

****

Palmer was glad to get off the plane; he wasn't a good traveller and the seats were always too narrow, and never had enough leg room which played hell with his sciatica. Next to him Gheeta had been quite comfortable, and spent the three hours flicking through various 'techie' magazines she had bought at Heathrow and then revising the case. In her civilian fawn Armani trouser suit, McQueen sneakers, Burberry shoulder bag and tinted Raybans, she looked about as far away from an English police officer as you could get as they walked through customs green channel. Designer clothes were

Gheeta's one weakness. The only visible change to Palmer's usual attire was that he was carrying his crombi rather than wearing it and was wearing an old pair of sandals that Mrs P. had insisted replace his black brogues for the trip. He had argued but she was adamant.

'You can't go on the beach in shoes.'

'We are not going on the beach. We are going on police business, not going on holiday.'

'It's the Canary Islands Justin, everybody wears sandals – it's thirty degrees out there. You'll look daft in shoes.'

So he gave in as he always did with Mrs P and wore the sandals, and he still looked daft. His trademark trilby stayed firmly in place – it would take a nuclear bomb to separate that from his head when he was working. He had once told Mrs P that he wanted that hat to be buried with him. She had replied that it was definitely going to be buried with him, together with as much of his wardrobe as she could squash into the casket with him. It would be a time capsule to 1950s fashion!

****

'There's our driver, over there, guv', said Gheeta, pointing to a young man in *Policia Local* uniform standing in amongst the row of taxi drivers and holding up a sign that said 'PELMAR'.

Palmer showed his warrant card and all three exchanged greetings as they followed the driver through the big exit doors out of the Arrivals Lounge to the taxi rank where a police car waited for them. Palmer was just about to climb in when he stopped.

'Hang on.'

He swung round to look back at the terminal building.

'Don't tell me you left something on the plane, guv?' said Gheeta from the other side of the car.

Palmer squinted, trying to see through the frosted plate glass into the Departures Lounge.

'That was Freddy Doorman, I'm sure it was. What's he doing here?'

THE END

TAKEAWAY TERROR

CHAPTER 1

Jack Bernard was just nineteen and was killed because of money. Not money he owed anybody, not money he had stolen. He was killed because he was trying to make a bit of extra money delivering take-aways in the evenings.

He and his moped were crushed by a hit and run, long wheel base Transit van as he parked up to make a late night delivery.

Jack was the third delivery boy to be killed that way in three months. Another two had managed to jump clear of the six-wheeled assassin just in time, unable to pursue it on their bikes which were rendered into a tangled mess of steel. The Transit was carrying false plates, with no lights and no markings.

****

DCS Palmer was fidgeting. He was hungry. It was Friday evening and he was home for once. The report files from his last case were completed that afternoon at his office at the Yard and were ready for the DPP office. His celebratory Chinese takeaway Mrs P. had ordered was on its way, although he knew that at any moment the phone could ring, and it would end up inside Daisy – his faithful English Springer – rather than on his plate which was warming in the oven. Daisy was curled up by his feet, hoping the phone would ring and hoping the meal had beef in it. Palmer rose from the sofa and looked expectantly out of the windows, hoping to see the delivery lad coming up the front garden path of his Dulwich Village home. No such luck.

'Give them a ring and ask them where it is. They don't usually take this long,' he called over his shoulder to Mrs P. who was arranging two trays in the kitchen ready for the meal. She didn't really like eating off trays with the telly on as Palmer always managed to spill some of it down his front or onto the carpet as he concentrated on the TV and not getting his fork into his mouth, but it was a bit of a ritual this Friday night takeaway in the Palmer house.

Mrs P. did the week's shopping on a Friday afternoon. No supermarkets in Dulwich Village, so she usually drove to Brixton or Streatham and timed her return to coincide with Palmer arriving home; that was if he wasn't off chasing a serial killer somewhere. She would order their takeaway and together they would put the shopping away, open a bottle of

Argentinian Marbec and relax with the meal in front of the TVand watch one of the cheap games shows that run on TV at that time of day. Well, she would *try* to watch whilst Palmer interrupted her concentration continually with his comments: 'Who's he?', 'Never heard of him' and 'Mutton dressed as lamb!' which he aimed at the Z-list celebrities who seemed to populate the game shows at that early evening time.

'I expect they are busy,' Mrs P. shouted back. 'It's Friday night after all. Oh, and by the way – make sure you are home next Saturday evening.'

'Why?'

He picked up the paper and checked the TV listings in case Sky had a decent football match on. Probably not. Since they'd lost the Spanish contract he'd had to make do with the Premier League; it was okay, but he'd rather watch Barcelona than Huddersfield Town.

'It's Benji's sixtieth, he's having a do at the local pub. Booked the function room, and we are invited.'

'I'm working.'

This was Palmer's standard answer to anything involving his neighbour Benji.

'No you are not. You never work on Saturdays unless you have to.'

'I have to next Saturday.'

'Why?'

'Because it's Benji's sixtieth and I don't want to go. It will be full of local councillors and Benji's old mates, that Pride lot.'

'LGBT.'

'What?'

'That's the correct term, not *that Pride lot* – LGBT.'

'I thought that was a sandwich?' said Palmer with a cheeky twinkle in his eye.

'That's BLT, and no you didn't think that at all. Next Saturday evening, keep it free. I'll be most disappointed if you don't make it, and so will Benji. You may not realise it, but he really respects you.'

'It'll be vegetarian eats, won't it? All lentils and bits of hedgerow.'

'Just be there Justin Palmer, or else.'

Benji – real name Benjamin- was Palmer's nemesis, as well as his next-door neighbour: a retired advertising agency executive in his mid-fifties – single and with a massive pension, and nothing to spend it on except world cruises and new cars – he was the opposite of Palmer. A fake tan, ponytail and designer clothes completed the image, and his flamboyant manner and mincing walk had Palmer unsure of Benji's sexuality, although he would never make reference to it on the explicit instructions of Mrs P. But what really got under Palmer's skin, although he would never admit it, was that all the women of Dulwich Village – well, those of a certain age from the WI and Church Flower Arrangement Brigade, who had previously flirted and paid attention to Palmer – had transferred to Benji almost as soon as he moved in; and when he recently stood for the council it was their block votes that put him top of the poll and elected him.

In the last two years, Benji's top-of-the-range garden hot tub – big enough to float the Titanic – had burst and flooded Palmer's front garden, and then Benji's latest barbecue, which was about as big as Palmer's kitchen, had toppled over and burnt down part of the dividing fence. But, for all that, Palmer liked the man; and yes, he'd try and be there for the sixtieth birthday.

The doorbell rang. At last, food had arrived.

Mrs P. came into the lounge.

'Give me twenty pounds.'

'How much?' Palmer asked, feigning shock.

'Twenty pounds. We have the same meals every time and it's always twenty pounds, and you always say *how much*. You know how much – eighteen for the meal, two for the delivery boy. Twenty pounds please.'

She held out her hand

'Where are we getting it from, Harrods?'

'You say that every time too.'

He pulled a twenty from his pocket and she hurried off down the hall to the door. He tossed the paper aside, not having found anything worth watching on TV, as usual. Thank goodness for Netflix and Sky. He resented paying the BBC licence fee, especially since the disclosure of the hundreds of thousands of pounds some of the presenters got for reading an auto cue, so he clicked over to Netflix. He could usually find a decent film or Mafia series on there to watch.

He settled back as Mrs P. put their food on the plates in the kitchen and brought it through on trays.

'He said there was another delivery chap in a road accident earlier in the West End. Three in a month been killed by hit and run.'

'Blimey, dangerous job then.'

Palmer was more interested in his meal than in hit and runs. He was just about to spoon a sweet and sour prawn ball into his mouth when the phone rang. He swore blind he could see a smile cross Daisy's face.

****

CHAPTER 2

'What did you say his name was?'

'Jack Bernard.'

Palmer nodded and turned the collar of his thick overcoat up, as protection against the cold rain that seemed to be coming at him horizontally. He pulled the front of his trilby down a bit to keep it out of his face. He was stood looking at the wreckage of Jack Bernard's moped, flattened against the tarmac road. Eight foot-high crime scene screens had been erected around three sides of it and a tarpaulin strung across the top to keep the rain off; crime scene cordon tape was stretched across the street twenty yards either way from the scene. Next to him Chief Inspector Longman from West End Central uniform branch stood bent against the rain and wished he had brought his raincoat with him from the station when the uniformed traffic patrol had called in the accident. He wanted to turn the scene over to Palmer as soon as he could and get back to the shelter of the station.

'Where's the body?' asked Palmer as he bent close to the wreckage and saw some blood stains on the tarmac.

'Taken to West End Central morgue.'

Behind them a brand-new top-of-the-range black Range Rover silently pulled up outside the cordon tape and DS Gheeta Singh slipped out of the front passenger door as a smart looking young man exited the driver's side. They stopped at the tape, where Singh showed her ID card to the two officers who were keeping the public and press photographers at a distance. They allowed her through and she stooped under the tape and walked to Palmer, who introduced her to DCI Longman.

'DS Singh, meet CI Longman from West End Central. Singh is my number two,' he explained.

That was a bit of a shortened bio of DS Singh, as not only was she his number two in the Serial Murder Squad but he had pulled strings and called in old favours to get her there. After seeing her at work in the Cyber Crime and IT Unit, he had decided she was just what his department needed to get it updated and kept abreast of the rapidly changing face of crime in this era of social media.

Singh was in a designer trouser suit and patent shoes. She'd obviously had been out at a social event when her beeper had alerted her to ring in to the Yard, who had told her that

Palmer had asked for her presence at the scene. Palmer noted the young man left at the tape.

'Hope I didn't disturb anything important? 'he said, raising his eyebrows and flashing a knowing smile.

Gheeta smiled back.

'Well, we will never know now guv, will we?'

She walked over and spoke to the young man, who went to the car and came back with a raincoat and helped her put it on. Then she gave him a peck on the cheek, before he returned to the car and drove off.

Palmer had noted that even coming from an evening out Gheeta had her laptop in its case slung over her shoulder. He couldn't remember the last time he'd seen her without it, the reason being that she could tap into their mainframe and servers at the Squad Office in Scotland Yard on wi-fi and download any information they might need within minutes from their data banks.

'Right then guv, what have we here then?'

She flipped up the rain hood on the coat, took the laptop from its satchel and started taking pictures of the scene. Palmer looked to CI Longman to explain. Longman cleared his throat, resigned himself to another few minutes in the rain, and spoke.

'Well, being the third fatality of a delivery boy and having had two other similar hit and runs that just crushed the bikes, it's pretty obvious to us that there's a war going on somewhere. What sort of war we don't know, but I can't imagine that there's enough money in takeaway meals to murder for, so it could be drugs – witnesses have described the same vehicle doing the damage at each scene so it's not random hit and runs. And seeing that my CID is overstretched already with the wave of knife crime and your department is tooled up to take on serial killings, I have great pleasure in handing over to you.'

He gave Palmer a false smile.

'Have fun.' And with that he was off.

He didn't get far. Palmer and Singh exchanged glances, then Palmer shouted loudly and in a superior voice after Longman:

'Just one minute, Chief Inspector!'

Longman stopped and turned. Palmer's face showed he was not amused.

'You *will* have a full report of the other deaths and all the witness statements and attending officers' notes through to my Sergeant tomorrow, won't you.'

It was a statement not a question. Longman realised he'd taken on the wrong person to be so abrupt with. He smiled a false smile to each of them.

'Yes, yes of course,' he said, standing like a scolded schoolboy.

Palmer shooed him away with a wave of his hand.

'Good. Right then, off you go – we will take it from here.'

Longman nodded and was gone, his tail between his legs. Palmer looked at Singh.

'How do twats like that get to be Chief Inspectors, eh?'

Singh diplomatically didn't answer, noticing the smiles the uniformed officers at the cordon tape exchanged with each other as Longman left. She stooped over the mangled remains and looked at the moped's wooden carrier box, now splintered on the road.

'Why would anybody do this, guv? Longman's got to be right on one thing though, I can't believe there's enough money in delivering takeaways to warrant it. The carrier box is empty, so he'd already delivered the meal. If the killer wanted to disrupt the business, surely he'd kill him before the delivery was made.'

Palmer gave himself a small smile. Singh was already exploring the whys and wherefores and they hadn't even seen the reports yet. He liked that approach.

'Now, now, Sergeant, let's not run before we can walk. Let's get all the information and reports and take a good look before we go into the reasons – plenty of time for that tomorrow. Nothing we can do here. Come on.'

They started to walk to the squad car.

'I don't know about you but I'm starving – I had two mouthfuls of a Chinese meal when the call came. I expect it's inside the dog now.'

'You can't feed that to the dog, guv!'

'Oh, well it's inside Mrs P. then. One thing's for sure, she wouldn't have thrown it away. How was your evening going?'

'We'd just sat down in an Italian place I've been meaning to try for ages. Just ordered.'

'That's the nature of the job, eh? Who's the lad, new boyfriend?'

'First date.'

'Oh dear. Well, it will be a test to see if he's keen.'

Down the road a car flashed its headlights and the black Range Rover pulled out from the kerb and pulled up beside them. Gheeta's date smiled across as Palmer opened the passenger door for her and ushered her in with a bow.

'He's keen', he said to her quietly out of the side of his mouth. 'See you in the morning, Sergeant. Don't rush to get in 'cause we can't do anything until we get those reports.'

He gave her a wink, closed the door and made for his squad car.

****

CHAPTER 3

'Right then, what have we got?'

Palmer stood and paced the room. It was mid-afternoon the next day and in the Team Room at the Yard Palmer and DS Singh had been reading through the reports on the hit-and-runs, highlighting the relevant facts for Claire – their civilian Technical Clerk – to input into the mainframe server: names, times, routes, addresses, and all sorts of what might seem to be irrelevant facts that the computer programmes would sort and sift through, looking for a thread. Palmer's favourite word *was thread*. He knew that in every serial murder case there would be one *thread*, if not more than one, and that thread or threads would tie the killings together and hopefully point him to the killer.

'Three deaths, two near misses, an unidentified murder vehicle, and not much else.'

Gheeta sat back in her chair.

'None of the victims had any previous other than parking tickets, which you might expect considering the work they did. They all worked in the gig economy, getting paid for each delivery, and the deliveries were for a number of different fast food outlets and restaurants.'

'But, their calls were all routed to them through the same work hub,' Claire added. 'A delivery service called Deliver- Eat.'

Palmer nodded.

'Right, then that would seem to be our first call. You two won't remember it but about thirty years ago we had a mini-cab war in London – same sort of set up, drivers paying a weekly fee to the company for their calls. That ended up with cabs being smashed up and fire bombs chucked into offices. Could be we've got the start of something similar here.'

'Cold-blooded murder is a bit heavier than smashing up cars and offices, guv – there's got to be more to this than just delivering meals. I still think there can't be enough money in that to kill for.'

'Drugs?' Claire asked.

'Could be,' Palmer pondered. 'One thing you noted last night Sergeant that needs to be explained is why were the delivery boys hit after the delivery? If you wanted to disrupt a delivery service surely you'd hit them before they delivered to annoy the customers?'

'So whoever did it either wanted to keep the customer happy, or didn't want us – the police – to get hold of the meal?' said Gheeta.

'Or the drugs,' said Claire.

'Or both,' Palmer added. 'I think a visit to this Deliver- Eat place is definitely needed. Give them a call and tell them we are coming.'

****

The Deliver-Eat offices were in a modern business centre off the Edgware Road. A smart single-storey glass-fronted unit gave the visitor an inside view of a typical call centre layout: rows of desks with phone operators busy taking calls and using computer keyboards and screens in front of them.

Palmer and Singh left their squad car in the 'visitors only' parking space and walked through the automatic sliding double glass doors into a reception area. They were obviously expected as the young brunette receptionist in her 'Deliver- Eat' monogrammed jacket made her way from behind the counter and welcomed them.

'You must be Superintendent Palmer, sir. We are expecting you.'

She smiled warmly.

'Detective *Chief* Superintendent Palmer actually,' he corrected her. 'And this is Detective Sergeant Singh.'

221

He smiled warmly back. Gheeta felt a trifle embarrassed for the receptionist; she had heard him correct so many people about his proper rank that she had lost count. His excuse for doing so was that it had taken him over fifty years to get to the rank, and he was damn well going to have people use it.

'Would you follow me please,' said the receptionist, a little flustered. She led them through more double glass sliding doors into the call centre itself, then along a central path between the rows of telephonists' desks and through yet another set of double doors to the control area, where a dozen dispatchers with headphones and screens gave out the jobs taken in the Centre whilst watching a giant map of London on a screen that took up the whole of the end wall. Numbered lights were flashing on it, some red and some green.

A middle-aged portly man in shirtsleeves and with a receding hairline detached himself from the area and came over, removing his glasses and putting them in his Deliver-Eat shirt pocket. The receptionist carefully announced Palmer.

'This is *Detective Chief* Superintendent Palmer and Detective Sergeant Singh.'

She turned to them.

'This is Daniel Court, our CEO.'

They shook hands and exchanged pleasantries. Court indicated a very modern leather button sofa and chairs away in a quiet corner and they sat down.

'Would you like a coffee or tea?' Court offered.

Palmer waved the offer away.

'No, no, thank you, we won't take up much of your time as I'm sure you've been through all this before with the local police.'

Court looked sad and shook his head.

'Yes, not a very nice thing to happen. Jack was a good lad. A good worker, one of our best.'

'I noticed the report we got from the local force didn't give his work rota for the evening he was killed. Would you have a copy we might look at, with the addresses he delivered to and at what times?'

'He wasn't working that night.'

'He wasn't?'

'No.'

'But he was on his Deliver-Eat moped and seen to take a meal into an apartment block before the incident happened.'

223

'Maybe he was working for some other service, or a local takeaway. It wasn't *our* moped – we only provide the insulated food box on the back. Our delivery people use their own bikes and mopeds. No, he definitely wasn't working for us that night, he only did four evenings a week for us. He could have had more, but only wanted the four.'

'I see.'

Palmer thought for a moment.

'Could we have a copy of any paperwork you might have on the lad? Application form, that sort of thing.'

'Of course.'

'And the same for the other two chaps who were killed, and the two who managed to jump out of the way.'

'None of them worked for us.'

'Really? We weren't aware of that.'

'No, lots of takeaways have their own staff doing their deliveries.'

Gheeta pointed to the big screen.

'Is each of those numbered lights a delivery person?'

'They are, yes. Green light for 'on a delivery', red for 'available'.

'Lots of them, aren't there? How many do you have out there?'

'Just over two hundred at any one time during the day, and up to four hundred on the weekends and evenings. We have one dispatcher for every twenty on call.'

Gheeta pointed to the rows of operators in the main room.

'So, a call comes in for a delivery to be made by phone, and I presume the telephonist that receives it fills in a standard template on their computer, which is sent on your intranet system to the dispatcher controlling the team covering that area?'

'Correct. It's programmed by postcode, and that dispatcher then sends it through to the nearest available bike in or near that postcode.'

'By wi-fi?'

'Yes, each delivery person has a company app on their mobile that receives the details. Then their number on the screen turns to red once they acknowledge they have received the job, and then back to green once the job is completed.'

'You have a backup system?'

'Of course.'

'So, should we want to have a printout of Jack Bernard's jobs for that week you could extract it from the backup system of the intranet?'

'Yes.'

Palmer had no idea what the devil his Sergeant was talking about, but her IT knowledge never ceased to amaze him; so he sat back and let her carry on, nodding now and again as though he knew exactly what she was talking about.

'That's good,' Gheeta smiled contentedly. 'Okay, then I would be grateful if you would get your system manager to send us the complete work history for Jack over the last three months.'

She gave Court one of her cards.

'Send it to that email please.'

Court looked at the card for a moment or two.

'I'm not sure we can do that. Data protection and all that.'

Palmer bristled. There was nothing he hated more than somebody putting a barrier in the way of an investigation by quoting stupid rules and regulations.

'Oh I think you can manage that, sir. The alternative would be for me to get a warrant to seize the dispatchers' computers for forensic analysis – and maybe I'd come and seize then on a Friday evening.'

He raised his eyebrows questioningly at Court.

'How would that suit you?'

'I'll have those work records to you within an hour.'

Palmer smiled.

'Very helpful of you, sir.'

He stood and buttoned his coat.

'We won't detain you any longer, Mr Court. I am sure young Bernard's family will be very grateful for the help you have given us in trying to find their son's murderer.'

He gave Court a sharp look and Gheeta followed him out to the squad car.

'Well, that's a turn up for the books,' said Palmer as they settled into the rear passenger seats. 'So who was Jack Bernard working for on that night then, eh? '

'Why would he bother to work for another delivery service when more work was on offer at Deliver-Eat?' Gheeta asked.

'Better money?'

'If that was the case, he'd work there all the time and ditch Deliver-Eat, wouldn't he? But surely Deliver-Eat is one of the biggest so they must at least pay as much as any other to keep their staff; and there's only so much profit in a takeaway meal to pay a delivery lad from.'

'Perhaps it wasn't a meal that he was delivering, guv.'

'Yes, that's looking more and more likely isn't it? I think I'll ask Reg Frome to take a look at the mangled bike and box. Ask Claire to send him through the details with a forensic report request in the morning.'

****

CHAPTER 4

'Well, well, well. Justin Palmer you old devil, you got that one spot on.'

Reg Frome stood up from his kneeling position in the large Evidence Warehouse at West End Central and placed the swab he had used on the remnants of the Deliver-Eat box from Bernard's moped into an evidence bag. The swab was blue; it started out white, but even the most miniscule amount of cocaine would turn it blue.

Reg Frome was head of Forensics in the Murder Squad umbrella, and that included Palmer's Serial Murder Squad as well as Organised Crime and Anti-Terrorism. Both he and Palmer had graduated from Hendon Police College at the same time many years before; Frome had chosen forensics and Palmer had stuck to his preferred police work. Both were now at the top of their tree and fighting early retirement offers from above in the annual pruning of the budget. Their respect was mutual, as was their ribbing of each other.

He dialled Palmer's mobile number. Palmer answered with his usual one word.

'Palmer.'

'Blue is the colour,' sang Frome into the phone. Being a lifelong Chelsea supporter, and Palmer being the same for Arsenal, he took every opportunity to stick one in.

Palmer laughed.

'Good morning, Reg. So I take it we have a positive?'

'We do indeed. Three swabs in the Deliver-Eat box, or the pieces that are left of it, and everyone of them giving a positive.'

'We had our suspicions.'

'The Duty Officer here says they have the other two wrecks in storage from the other hit-and-runs where the lads were killed. Want me to do them whilst I'm over here?'

'Yes, I was thinking that. Might as well if you don't mind, Reg. Ten to one on you get positives.'

****

CHAPTER 5

Sammy Wellbeck stood in the middle of his Hackney scrapyard and watched as the remains of a Fiat were hauled into the air by a magnetic crane and dropped into the crusher that devoured it like a predator on its prey, until it became a six foot by three foot square metal oblong that was picked up again by the crane and stacked together with a heap of others waiting to go off to the smelter's.

Business was good, especially since the government car tax rises on diesel cars. Motorists were chipping them in as part exchange for petrol or hybrid cars to dealers who knew they had no chance of selling them on, and were quite happy for the likes of Sammy Wellbeck to clear their yards once a month paying half scrap weight. And that price didn't account for the saleable parts Sammy's mechanics stripped off them.

Sammy's yard was big. It had a large corrugated warehouse with aisles of tall shelves holding everything a motorist might want for their car, from engines and doors to nuts and bolts; and all at considerably lower prices than they cost new. The counter was open on a Saturday only and was always busy; the money was always cash.

Next to the warehouse a good-sized brick and tile single-storey office block housed reception and Sammy's large office. Clean, tidy and presentable, it was chalk and cheese to the warehouse, but that was because Sammy's wife Chrissie ran that side of the business: the reception, the accounts, the payouts and most importantly, the books. In fact she ran two sets of books – one set for HMRC and VAT, and one set with the true figures.

The perimeter of Sammy's yard was a twenty foot-high double brick wall with razor wire along the top. The large double door entrance was three inch steel on rollers with a Judas door in one corner. CCTV scoped the yard, the walls, the outside of the entrance and the approaching backstreet. The reason his warehouse was only open to the public on a Saturday was that Sammy didn't like uninvited visitors, as he had other business to do during the week.

Sammy Wellbeck was a narco – a drug dealer. A major drug dealer…

****

CHAPTER 6

In the team room Gheeta pinned up the mugshots of the deceased on the progress chart and below each one a police picture of the crushed moped. Something in her brain was making alarm signals. Something wasn't right; almost like the computer programmes she wrote on crime comparison that disseminated all the information she and Claire input, her brain was flagging an error. And she was looking at it.

She turned to where Palmer was reading the newly arrived forensic reports.

'Guv, that manager at Deliver-Eat said that only Bernard worked for them, didn't he? The other two victims didn't work for Deliver-Eat did they?'

Palmer carried on reading as he answered.

'That's what he said, yes.'

Gheeta checked the pictures again.

'So how come they had Deliver-Eat boxes on their bikes?'

Palmer put down the reports and joined Gheeta at the progress chart.

'Did they?'

He peered closely at the broken remains of the bikes and boxes.

233

'They did, didn't they.'

'Somebody is telling porkies, guv.'

Palmer thought for moment.

'Do we have any pictures of the bikes belonging to the other two lads, the ones who weren't injured?

'No, I assume they recovered them themselves. Could be for the insurance claim.'

Palmer gave her a '*don't be silly*' look.

'You don't think either of them – or for that matter most of the delivery lads in London – actually have insurance, do you? Or road tax?'

Gheeta clicked her tongue.

'Guv, you always assume the worst in people.'

'Forty-five years in this job tells me it's a good place to start, Sergeant.'

'Shall I pay another visit to Mr Court?'

'No, if he or somebody in his organisation is using couriers to deliver coke we don't want to let them know we are treating this as more than hit-and-runs just yet. I think we might pay a visit to the three victims' relatives and see what they have to say. Should be interesting.'

****

The Walworth Estate off the Elephant and Castle was much like most other council estates: pockets of well-cared-for houses with well-tended if small front gardens, and pockets of run-down, uncared-for distressed houses and flats; the former more likely remnants of Thatcher's Right to Buy incentive, and the latter still in the social housing sector reliant on the cash-strapped council for upkeep.

Gheeta rang the bell on the Bernards' front door. She and Palmer had come in a marked police car with a driver who stayed in the car. Palmer liked to cover his back in these estates and liked to have a pair of eyes outside, just in case. In the seventies when he was a young detective venturing into these estates to make an arrest with other officers, their presence would be signalled by the banging of dustbin lids or blowing of whistles, warning the local villains to hide last night's loot and any absconders around to disappear fast. These days it was the mobile phone that passed on notification of their presence, warning the dealers to hide their drugs or move it quickly off the estate. Amazing the number of innocent-looking little old ladies pulling shopping trolleys that suddenly made for the exits when police came on the estates.

Jack Bernard's mother was a widow in her mid-forties, sharp-faced with little make-up and plain dressed in a grey trouser suit and trainers. She had a tidy semi in a good part of the estate and invited them in; they were expected, as Gheeta had rung beforehand to arrange a convenient time.

They refused the offer of tea or coffee and sat in the kitchen.

'You do know I've been through all this before with the police, don't you? I can't think of anything I can add.'

Palmer turned on his *killer* smile, guaranteed to melt an iceberg.

'I know Mrs Bernard, and believe me the last thing we want to do is cause you further grief. The truth is that Jack was not the only delivery lad to have been targeted by that particular hit-and-run vehicle.'

'He wasn't?' she asked, dabbing a tear.

'No, nor the only fatality. Two other lads were killed and another two hit but managed to jump out of the way. So you see it puts a totally new scenario on the whole thing. It brings his death out of the hit-and-run accident scenario and into the realms of a serial murder case with Jack targeted, and that puts it firmly into my department's remit. So we will be starting again from the beginning and using all our experience in this area to bring the killer to book.'

'Oh my God, three of them.'

She was visibly shocked. Gheeta now took over.

'We have all the reports and case file documents from the original investigation, and if I might recap Jack worked for Deliver-Eat on various shifts delivering meals, mainly in the evenings?'

Mrs Bernard nodded positively. Gheeta continued.

'On that last day he left here to go to work as usual, yes?'

'Yes, evening shift. He went about five o-clock.'

'To work for Deliver-Eat?'

'Yes.'

'Did Jack work for any other delivery companies that you know of?'

'No.'

'Or maybe directly for another takeaway?'

'No, he liked his job and the company. They always treated him fairly so why would he move? He didn't earn a fortune but he did okay. He'd only just got a new scooter, his pride and joy.' She smiled at the recollection. 'It's at the police pound, or what's left of it is. I can't claim the insurance money until I get access to it for the insurance company man to look at it. Be handy money too, to pay off the funeral debt. Awful really, when you see your son off to work and you get back a body, a signet ring and his mobile.'

Palmer noticed Gheeta's eyes flash directly at Mrs Bernard. He also noticed how she tried to conceal an amount of excitement in her voice.

'Do you have Jack's mobile?'

'Yes, it's a bit crushed but I can still look through the photos. He liked taking selfies of himself with his mates and their scooters, or mopeds or whatever they're called.'

Gheeta gave a reassuring smile.

'Would it be possible for me to have a look at the phone? We won't be taking it away, but I might be able to find some new evidence.'

'Of course, just a minute.'

Mrs Bernard left the room.

'If the SIM card is intact guv, this could open up the case.'

'Yes, just what I was thinking,' lied Palmer, who had no idea what a SIM card was.

Gheeta gave him a raised eyebrow.

'Of course you were, guv.'

Palmer had brought Gheeta Singh into his squad purely because of her knowledge of cyber and IT and was quite prepared to give her the go-ahead on anything to do with those spheres of police work. Her knowledge and expertise had paid dividends in the past cracking open cases, and maybe she was onto something in this case.

Mrs Bernard returned with a rather battered mobile phone that she handed to Gheeta.

'Take it away if you think it will help.'

'Shouldn't need to, Mrs Bernard. Let's have a look.'

Gheeta flipped open the battery lid and pulled out the SIM card.

'That's all I need.'

She powered up her laptop, slipped the SIM card into one of the side USB ports and tapped away on the keyboard.

'That's good, it's all working perfectly. What I'll do, if I may, is copy the information now to work on back at the office, so I won't need to take it away and the phone will be just as it is now.'

'Yes, please do.'

Gheeta already had, and the information was downloaded in seconds. She took the SIM from the USB and put it back into the phone, which she passed back to Mrs Bernard.

'That's it, that's all we need.'

Palmer leaned forward and lay a reassuring hand on Mrs Bernard's arm.

'May I ask you a personal question, Mrs Bernard?'

'Of course.'

'Did Jack take drugs?'

Mrs Bernard's eyes widened aggressively.

'No, no he did not. He hated all that stuff, said he'd seen too many of his friends ruin their lives with drugs. No, he did not take drugs.'

Palmer nodded.

'Okay, just ticking off the boxes. We have to ask these questions, I'm afraid.'

He stood to go.

'Well, I think we have all we need to go on with, thank you Mrs Bernard. If you think of anything that might be relevant, just give my Sergeant a call please.'

He nodded to Sergeant Singh who passed Mrs Bernard a contact card. They expressed their condolences again and left.

The families of the other two victims were adamant that their sons worked for Deliver-Eat, which was surprising as Court had denied knowledge of them. This bemused Palmer as their phones both had the Deliver-Eat app installed. Gheeta downloaded their SIM information.

'Why would he do that, Sergeant? Why would Court deny they worked for him? Pretty obvious the apps would say otherwise?'

****

CHAPTER 7

The next morning in the Team Room Claire was uploading the forensic and pathology reports whilst Gheeta uploaded the contents of Jack Bernard's phone into a mainframe computer and set about searching it for clues. She scrolled down the contents until she found what she was looking for – the Deliver-Eat app – and opened it.

'Right then, let's see what we can find in here,' she murmured to herself.

Across the corridor in his office Palmer re-read the Crime Scene Officer reports from the three death scenes. There was one fact that was a constant and soon stood out. He finished his reading and walked across to the Team Room.

'How much is a normal takeaway meal, twenty quid for two?'

Claire answered without interrupting her inputting.

'No, that's a lot. We have an Indian every now and again and it's about twelve pounds, plus three for delivery.'

Palmer sat down in one of the government contract steel chairs in front of the progress board.

242

'And if a delivery lad delivered four an hour over a five hour shift, he'd take about three hundred quid in an evening.'

Claire turned away from her keyboard and laughed.

'They don't do it that way, sir. If you're having it delivered you pay by card on the phone when ordering.'

'Mrs P. pays by cash at the door.'

'They must know you as a reliable regular customer, not likely to be a hoax call. They get a lot of those and asking for card payment weeds them out.'

'I see. So for a delivery chap to have over three hundred pounds in his pocket would seem strange, wouldn't it?'

'Very strange. Why?'

'Well, according to the crime scene inventory all three of our victims had over three hundred notes in their pockets.'

He thought for a moment.

'Claire, give Mr Court at Deliver-Eat a call and ask if his lads collect money. Don't tell him why we want to know.'

He busied himself trying to find a comfortable way of sitting on the government contract steel chairs without starting up his sciatica whilst Claire made the call. He still wasn't comfortable when she came back with the answer.

'They don't collect any money at all. The only cash their delivery boys are allowed to accept is in the way of a tip.'

Palmer nodded.

'So, we have three lads killed, each with a bundle of cash in their pockets which can't be accounted for. Where did it come from?'

Gheeta sat back in her chair.

'I think I may have the answer, guv. Watch the screen.'

The large screen on the wall above the computer terminals lit up with the Deliver-Eat London street map.

'This is the street map off the hard drive I copied from their terminal at the Deliver-Eat offices.'

She tapped her keyboard.

'And this is the day Jack Bernard was killed. His call number was 102.'

The screen showed a myriad of numbers all over the screen.

'102 is not shown.'

'It was his day off, Court told us that,' said Palmer.

'Right, but if I overlay the details from Bernard's mobile app onto that map, it tells a different story.'

The number 102 added itself to the map in various locations.

'Bernard was indeed working, and he must have been working for Deliver-Eat because his jobs were being sent to his Deliver-Eat app.'

'His mum said he was working,' said Palmer.

Gheeta nodded.

'Yes she did, and she was right. He was getting jobs on his app from Deliver-Eat but they weren't registering on their big screen or on their system. Basically it is very simple to do – with a couple of clicks you can take 102 off the screen but continue to work him.'

'So somebody inside Deliver-Eat would have to do that?

'Yes.'

'Okay.'

Palmer stood up and rubbed his right thigh, the government contract steel chair having won in the sciatica battle. He knew the importance of Gheeta's words.

'We have somebody inside giving out non-registering jobs where money is collected. I think we all know where this is leading.'

Claire gave the answer they already knew.

'Drugs.'

'Give me five minutes guv,' Gheeta said, working her keyboard. 'I'll get a list of the addresses 102 – that is, Jack Bernard – picked up from and delivered to.'

'Okay, in the meantime I think I'll take a wander down to Organised Crime and have a word. Don't want to be treading on their toes, and this little scam looks to be very well organised.'

****

Commander Peter Long, head of Organised Crime at the Met, sat back in his chair and thought for a moment. His office was a glass cubicle in the corner of the OC Team Room. It was a busy room; it was a big department, with several teams working on several cases. Since Romania and Bulgaria had joined the EU and their citizens gained right of entry to the UK, organised gangs from those two countries had whooped with joy and expanded their drug routes across the channel to take advantage of the UK's growing population of cocaine- and heroin-dependent idiots.

'I think you should carry on with it, Justin,' Long said to Palmer sitting opposite. 'After all, it's a serial murder case which is your squad. And okay, it looks like drugs are involved, but they are involved in most crime these days, especially cocaine.'

He sighed.

'And I have more than enough on my plate with going after the big boys. You carry on, and give me a shout if you need help.'

Palmer nodded.

'Okay, but I need to cover my back with Bateman. I don't want him throwing a fit and saying I've exceeded my department's brief and should have handed it over to you as soon as I knew it was drug-related. So I'll copy you in on all our daily reports, keep you up-to-date.'

'Bateman is a pain in the arse.'

'We can agree on that.'

They both laughed. Assistant Commissioner Bateman was Senior Officer for both of their departments. A product of the fast-tracking from university programme instigated by the Home Office and never having had the experience of years on the beat and real interaction with criminals that Palmer and Long had behind them, he sat in his plush office on the fifth floor along with the other Assistant

Commissioners and Home Office liaison staff, pushing paperclips around his desk and coming up with even more paperwork that he viewed as necessary for the running of his department, but in truth just kept officers glued to their desks filling it out rather than out catching criminals.

His main purpose was keeping his departments within their prescribed budgets, and one of his aims was to integrate Palmer's Serial Murder Squad into Long's Organised Crime Squad, and then put both under the CID Office control and get rid of Palmer and Long. But when he came up with early retirement packages for them both, he met with two immovable objects; and such was the esteem that both were held with inside the force and with the political masters, he had to back down. Battle lines were drawn and regular skirmishes ensued.

'He will no doubt try to push this case over to you Peter, so be prepared.'

Long thought for a moment.

'But what if I'm already involved? Then he can't.'

'What do you mean?'

'If I have a man on your team working with you.'

Palmer gave a long smile. Long stood and opened his office door and called out into his team room.

'Knight! Come in here for a minute, will you?'

DS Knight looked up from inputting a case report onto his computer, shut it down and came over to the office. Long ushered him in and shut the door.

'DS James Knight, meet Detective Chief Superintendent Palmer, Serial Murder Squad.'

They shook hands.

'Heard a lot about you, sir,' said Knight. 'Nice to meet you.'

'Sit down, Knight.'

Long pulled a chair from the corner and put it by the desk. Knight sat down.

'How long will you be doing that case report?'

'Another hour or so.'

'And then?'

'DI Kirby wants me to do some discreet surveillance on a target for him.'

'Does he? Okay, forget that – you are going to work with the Serial Murder Squad. They have a case that would seem to be involving drug mules delivering under the guise of fast food deliveries. Three have been murdered. Seems to me that we could have somebody trying to get a foothold in somebody else's manor. You know all the main players in that game, so when you've finished your report get your things and join DCS Palmer upstairs. I'll clear it with Kirby. Happy with that?'

Knight was very happy with that.

'Yes sir'.

'Good. Off you go then.'

Knight left the office.

'He's a good officer, Justin. Been working on the drugs scene for three years – qualified firearms officer too. One of those I've in mind for promotion to team leader soon, competent and sensible. I want him back in one piece.'

Palmer rose to leave.

'If he's that good I might keep him.'

'You bloody won't. Now bugger off and catch a serial killer.'

****

CHAPTER 8

It was four in the afternoon when DS Knight appeared at the Team Room door. Palmer and Singh were putting Deliver-Eat details and Court's name on the progress board, linking them by felt tip to the three victims. Claire was gathering as much information on them and the two who escaped as she could find on police files and social media and inputting it into their databases in the hope some links might emerge.

Palmer did the introductions. Knight looked around the room.

'Where is everybody?'

Palmer laughed.

'This *is* everybody.'

'Three of you?'

'That's right. We don't have a case load like OC – serial killers are, thankfully, few and far between. But if needed I am allowed to pull in other officers to help or co-opt specialists, like yourself.'

He let Gheeta bring Knight up to speed with the facts so far. The most recent was the information she had pulled out from Bernard's Deliver-Eat app on the pick-up and delivery addresses for the day he was killed.

Palmer and Knight stood watching the big screen as she scrolled down the information.

'Ten different addresses he delivered to but only two pick-ups, both from the same place – 39 Glebe Street, just off the Charing Cross Road. I've checked it out, it's an Indian takeaway called The Curry Leaf.'

'Are you kidding?'

Knight looked very concerned as he glanced at Palmer.

'The Arif brothers.'

Palmer hadn't the slightest idea what he was on about.

'Who?'

'The Arif Brothers, sons of Turkish immigrants with middlemen drug supply contacts in that part of the world. They had a takeaway in Peckham with the same name, The Curry Leaf – ran a drugs empire covering South London from it. We hit them about six months ago; didn't get the brothers but put ten of their dealers inside. I can't believe they'd play the same game again.'

'Did they use the delivery lads?' Palmer asked.

'No, their dealers came to the place on a Friday evening under the guise of ordering a takeaway and bought enough drugs to supply their punters for the week. That's when we got them – sitting pretty in the back room with fifteen kilos of cocaine and a hundred and twenty thousand in cash.'

'But not the brothers.'

'No, too clever. They never get near to the operation, organise it all from burner phones. Fly it in from Europe to small or disused airstrips, or bring it over in small boats to marinas; then their people pick it up and take it to a safe house or a shop rented monthly for cash. They cut it, split it, and do the business with the middlemen who packet it and supply the street dealers.'

'So if the brothers got burnt for one hundred and twenty grand, they're not likely to use that system of distribution again, are they?'

'No, they won't. Too clever.'

'So Deliver-Eat would be an ideal cover for their runners to shift it from the premises to the middlemen.'

'Absolutely ideal.'

Gheeta pointed to the screen.

'So all these addresses that Jack Bernard went to could well be middlemen who package it for their teams of street dealers.'

Knight nodded.

'Probably are.'

Palmer sat down.

'Okay, it's not likely that these Arifs are hitting their own people; so we must have somebody else in the frame who wants the Arifs gone.'

'There are quite a few little gangs dealing around the West End and North London,' Knight carried on. 'Mostly postcode gangs – gangs who operate inside their own postcodes or council estates and violently defend their turf if anybody else tries to do any dealing on it. Hence the large numbers of knifings and shootings. As fast as we hit one lot and put them away, others take over. But this isn't any of them, this is big time. The Arifs have stepped across the Thames and stepped on the toes of the big boys here, and are being sent a nasty message: *pack up and get out or else.* I think there's only one lot who would be capable of that, and that is Sammy Wellbeck.'

Palmer shrugged.

'Name doesn't ring a bell.'

'Clever man is Sammy Wellbeck – and his wife Christine, known as Chrissie. Operates out of a big scrap yard and second-hand car parts business in Hackney. He won't show up on a crime data base anywhere.'

He had noticed Gheeta tapping in Wellbeck on her terminal. She sat back.

'You're right, he doesn't.'

'As I said, clever man. Started out with a used car dealership and made a lot of money with ringers – turning the clock back, welding the front and backs of insurance company write-offs together to make one good one. He cornered the market with the insurance companies by giving backhanders to their decision makers – backhanders on the back of threats.'

Palmer nodded.

'There's a few I've known do that. Sweeten the pill.'

Claire hadn't heard of it.

'How does that work then, sir?'

'Well, let's say the chap who gives out the contracts for getting rid of the insurance company's write offs – that is, the *decision maker* – is out on his own somewhere, maybe even just having lunch or a quiet pint. Somebody – or more usually, two people – puts a proposition to him that his company's write-offs will be sold to, for instance, this Wellbeck character's scrap yard at a certain price per vehicle. The decision maker might say *no*, or *I'll call the police.* Bad move. He then gets told where his children go to school, what evenings his wife goes to the gym or bingo or whatever. The threat is implied, but – here comes the sweetener – a bag of money is passed over with the promise that a similar amount will be given to him every month. So, a two-pronged attack: the threat to the family, and the cash in the bag – never fails as the amount in the bag is enough to tempt anybody. And the insurance for the criminal is usually a photo taken of the cash handover without the mark knowing, so should he ever not play ball or want to terminate the deal he's shown the snap and told that copies will go to his boss, the papers and the police.'

Claire took a deep breath.

'Clever, clever.'

Knight continued.

'My guess is that the Arifs thought the area was a sort of mish-mash of smaller gangs and didn't realise that those smaller gangs were all supplied by Wellbeck. He's bringing the stuff in and shifting it out to the middlemen, who cut and pack it in twists for the street and club dealers. If the Arifs have any sense they'll pack up and clear off back to their own manor. They'd be no match for Wellbeck – he's in the frame for three murders over the last five years, but nobody will talk, they're too afraid of the consequences, Wellbeck doesn't take prisoners. The only firm that could take on Wellbeck and have a chance of winning is the Adamsons, and if they fancied their chances they'd have had a go by now.'

Another new one on Palmer.

'Adamsons?'

Knight nodded.

'Crime family who work out of Clerkenwell, they basically run the City and East End. Three brothers – three very clever brothers; thought to have financed the Hatton Garden Safe Deposit job. Top man is Terry Adamson – only ever been nicked for Proceeds of Crime when he couldn't explain his millions; his wife paid the seven hundred thousand pound fine in used fifties in Tesco bags. Mark my words, if Wellbeck could be pushed out the Adamsons would have done it by now. If the Arifs were to take over Wellbeck's manor, the Adamsons would not be pleased; and with their reputation for violence and murder, the Arifs would have another war on their hands. As I said before, if they have any sense they'll pack up and go back south of the Thames.'

'But whether they stay or go, it doesn't make any difference to us,' said Palmer. 'Let's not forget we are after a serial killer, not a drug dealer. Our killer may well be a dealer, and if he is and we take him down all the better; but it's the serial killer we are after.'

He stood and stretched.

'Right, that will do for today. Thank you Knight, your input has been enlightening. We have a good suspect target in this Wellbeck character to take a look at tomorrow.

****

CHAPTER 9

The evening light was fading outside. Sammy Wellbeck stood at his office window in the scrapyard, thinking hard. He made a tall, gaunt-looking figure, with little hair left and brown-stained chain smoker's fingers. In his early fifties he really wasn't in the mood for a turf war; that was all behind him, in the past. He just wanted his quiet narco life style to continue unabated. And the fucking Arifs were spoiling that.

Behind him, his wife Chrissie stood behind the reception counter doing business with one of the young dealers from a local estate. She was ten years younger than Sammy, with a trim figure, dyed copper hair that ringed her white face and dressed in a smart trouser suit and jacket. His two lieutenants, as he called them, Harry O'Keefe and Marty Chaplin sat on comfy guest chairs and watched. Both men had been with Wellbeck since the early days of car dealing.

Chrissie scooped a tablespoon of cocaine from a plastic box and sifted it carefully onto a scale.

'There you go Jamil, one hundred grams.'

She poured it into a plastic bag, sealed it, and pushed it across the counter. Jamil was a third generation British-Pakistani. He took a wad of twenty pound notes from inside his expensive jacket and handed it across without a word. Chrissie took it and slid it out of sight behind the counter.

'I don't need to count it do I, Jamil? You know the amount and you've always been spot on in the past.'

She gave him a false smile.

'If it's short, we know where to find you.'

'It's all there.'

Sammy turned and came over to Jamil, putting an arm round the boy's shoulders.

'Tell me Jamil, have you been approached by anybody lately? Anybody offering to supply?'

Jamil shook his head.

'No, Mr Wellbeck. Why?'

'Nothing really, just that we heard somebody might be around the district offloading a dodgy supply – Colombian low-grade mixed with some poisonous fertiliser. You sure you haven't heard a whisper?'

'Not heard nothing about that. Heard about a couple of new dealers on mopeds had showed up. Heard that you took care of them.'

He gave Wellbeck a large grin.

'Me?' Wellbeck said, feigning surprise. 'Come now Jamil, would I do anything like that?'

Jamil tilted his head and shrugged, the grin still in place. Wellbeck patted him on the back.

'Jamil, you just remember this: I look after my dealers, I make sure they aren't troubled. We are watching your back, Jamil. Our business, the business between you and me, it's based on loyalty. Just remember that, son.'

He gave him another pat on the back.

'Harry will walk you out. See you next week.'

Harry O'Keefe prised his bulk off the chair and opened the office door for Jamil, then followed him out across the yard to the Judas gate. He slipped the bolt and Jamil disappeared through it into the gloom. Sammy, Chrissie and Marty watched it happen on the CCTV screens in the office. Harry returned to the office and settled back into the chair. Chrissie took a drawer full of bank notes from behind the counter and started to count and band them into one-thousand-pound bundles. Sammy paced up and down a couple of times.

'Are they fucking stupid? If we'd had three of our blokes killed, we'd be at war.'

'They'd never win a war with us, boss,' O'Keefe said, a smile crossing his obese face. Five feet six and eighteen stone – people didn't mess with Harry O'Keefe. 'The Reilly's tried that didn't they, and they ran in the end.'

Wellbeck nodded. He remembered the Reilly gang trying to elbow into his manor some years ago. It was nasty, very nasty: bodies in the canal – some found, some not – dealer's homes fire bombed.

'We don't want to get into all that again'

Chrissie stopped counting and looked up.

'Strikes me you've got into that already. We've hit three of their delivery boys and crushed another two's bikes, and still they carry on. They ain't going anywhere, Sammy. What if they make our dealers an offer they can't refuse? What if they cut the price to below us and our dealers start to buy off them, eh? We have to hit them now – blow their fucking takeaway up, preferably with them inside it.'

O'Keefe murmured agreement. He liked his work; he liked hurting people, it gave him great pleasure. If your name was Sammy Wellbeck and you needed to control a manor, you needed a 'Harry O'Keefe' type to keep any upstarts under control, and fear is the best method of control man invented.

'I can run down a couple more? If their delivery blokes ain't got the message with three whacked, perhaps a couple more might do it?'

Marty Chaplin shifted uneasily in his chair. He was older than the others and in his late sixties. Always a smart dresser, he liked expensive suits and was well-groomed, with his dyed jet black hair slicked back giving him a vintage look.

'Be like the minicab wars of the old days, bloody offices being torched and cars being smashed up. I don't fancy going through that again.'

Chrissie scowled.

'If we hit them hard now, we won't have to go through anything will we, eh? Drug Squad kicked their arse over the other side of the river so they think they can just walk in here and start over? No way.'

'Maybe we could do a deal?' Chaplin offered.

Chrissie laughed.

'Oh yeah, we do a deal and all the other gangs see that and think they'll barge in on part of our manor and get a deal too, eh? The word would be out that the Wellbecks have gone soft and they'll be queuing up. No deals, no.'

Sammy turned to face them.

'She's right, you know. We have to hit them so hard they fuck off quick. You have to think of the message it would give to our suppliers if we don't. They'll think that maybe the Arifs are a better firm to back than us, and if that happens and they cut our supplies, or start feeding the Arifs, then we are done for.'

He paused for thought.

'Give Ronny Robards a call and get him to pop in.'

Marty Chaplin's heart sank. Everything had been tickety-boo; the business was good, the money coming in was more than enough, and after years of dodging the police and several stints in prison it had finally gone right, or as right as it ever could for a petty villain turned major name. And now, if Sammy wanted *Ronny Robards* to 'pop in' it was all going to turn nasty, very nasty.

Ronny Robards was an explosives man – Marty hoped Ronny was out of the business now, but doubted if he was. The same age as Marty, Ronny had built his reputation on opening safes with a bang when all else failed. The Wellbecks had used his expertise to secure the lucrative mini-cab trade of north London back in the sixties by literally 'blowing' the competition away. Ronny Robards's skills were so advanced that the police knew at once he was involved by their use.

Not for Ronny was the usual two pounds of Semtex slapped on the safe lock, light the fuse, go out of the building, wait for the bang and then go back and find the safe door swinging open, offering its riches on a plate; that didn't work, as Chubb and the other safe makers increased the security and anti-blast capabilities of their products. So Ronny increased his skills to keep ahead of them. He found a natural ability in his head to understand the new time lock systems and how to overcome them. He did break-ins to various safe makers' offices to steal their drawings, which he studied to find the weakest parts of their products. For a number of years his method of blasting the door hinges rather than the plated steel-reinforced lock systems paid dividends, until the companies realised their blunder. But in the end it just got too difficult and Ronny retired – or shall we say, semi-retired. He still provided the occasional package to a firm robbing a warehouse or jewellers that had not updated their safe or entry systems to withstand a blast.

Marty Chaplin knew exactly why Sammy had asked for Ronny to 'pop in'. The Arif takeaway was going to be torched.

****

CHAPTER 10

'We need some corroborative statements.'

Palmer, Knight and Singh sat at a table in the Team Room the next morning. Claire was still cross-referencing on the mainframe to try and link names and addresses.

'Have a trip round to the ones that got away,' Palmer continued. 'See if you can get one to talk and point the finger.'

Knight raised his eyebrows.

'We will be lucky if they do. If you'd had three mates killed and an attempt on your life, would you talk?'

Gheeta saw it another way.

'It would be a way of stopping *another* attempt on you, wouldn't it? Giving up the killer?'

'Another one would take his place. This is the organised drugs game – put a couple of thousand street dealers in jail, and there's another couple of thousand on the street taking their place within hours. I've known dealers refuse to name their suppliers even when offered Witness Protection. This game is run on fear, and that fear is backed up with violent actions.'

'Then there's the tie in with Deliver-Eat,' Palmer said. 'That's the key. Court's in this somewhere along the line, he can't claim ignorance now we have the proof of his company's involvement via the app. I think we ought to pay Mr Court another visit.'

****

They took a plain squad car from the car pool and Knight drove them to the Deliver-Eat premises. Palmer didn't want to be *announced* in any way, so they parked it around the corner out of sight.

'Okay, this is the plan. I will go in and collar Court; we've enough circumstantial on him, plus his lies about the victims not working for him to make an arrest. But I want to rinse him a bit first. I didn't get the impression he is a criminal type, so I think he's got dragged into this caper somehow and a bit of pressure will crack him. Give me five minutes to get at him and then you two bring the car round and wait in reception.'

He left the car and walked into the building, where the receptionist smiled in recognition as he approached her.

'Detective *Chief* Superintendent Palmer to see Mr Court,' he said, showing his warrant card.

'Is he expecting you?' came the reply as she ran her finger down an open day diary, but whether he was or wasn't didn't really matter. Palmer was already past her, through the glass doors and halfway down the main call centre floor before she could buzz Court's phone, and he was into the despatch area before Court knew he was on the premises.

Court was standing in front of the giant wall screen and turned to answer the internal phone which buzzed as Palmer entered.

'I wouldn't bother to answer that, Mr Court. It will be your receptionist announcing my arrival.'

Court looked out towards the reception, where the girl just shrugged in defeat. He raised a worried smile.

'Mr Palmer, I thought you had all you needed from us? This is an unexpected visit.'

'Really?'

Palmer was showing his nasty face, the one Mrs P. said could make the Pope feel guilty.

'An unexpected visit, eh? I would think it would be more an *expected* visit after the lies you told me before.'

He pointed to the sofa and chairs away in the corner.

'Sit down, Mr Court.'

He could see from Court's expression and non-answer that he'd been right; Court was in it up to his neck. Court sat on the sofa and Palmer remained standing a few feet in front of him, the power position favoured by interrogators.

'So, Mr Court, you told me Jack Bernard was off on the day he was killed; and that Hanson and Clark didn't work for you.'

Court was flustered.

'I want my lawyer.'

'Well you're not in custody, so you're not going to get him.'

Court made to get up and Palmer pushed him back down.

'Your choice, Mr Court. Sit and listen, or I arrest you, put handcuffs on you and march you out of the building in front of all your employees. Your choice.'

Court chose to stay seated and listen.

'Good, now let me bring you up to date. My Sergeant, who you met, is a very capable forensic computer analyst. We have the Deliver-Eat SIM card from Jack Bernard's mobile phone which puts him working on the day of his murder and taking calls from this office; calls that had him picking up from the same address twice. Once he'd picked up he then made numerous deliveries, presumably dropping off whatever it was he had picked up. Now, your clever little system of blanking out his 102 number from the screen doesn't blank it out from the hard drive memory – my clever sergeant brought it back to life, and hey presto! There is all the information on it that we need for me to call you a liar, for me to suspect you are involved in three murders, and for me to arrest you. And when my officers visited Hanson and Clark's bereaved families we found your apps on both their SIM cards, showing they too were working for you on the days they met their end. And they probably picked up from the same address Bernard did.'

He leaned in close to Court.

'So, Mr Court, I want the truth and I want it now, or you can kiss the family goodbye – if you have one – and look forward to spending the next thirty years in an eight by twelve foot cell with a variety of unsavoury characters for company. Take a couple of seconds to think about that before you say anything else.'

Court knew he was on a hiding to nothing.

'I'll do a deal.'

Palmer rolled his eyes at the ceiling and laughed.

'A *deal*? I think you've been watching too many American gangster films. You have nothing to offer me for a *deal*.'

'I can name names.'

'I already have the names. I assume you mean the Arifs?'

Court felt like he'd been hit with a sledgehammer.

'I had to do it, I don't have a choice.'

'Why?'

He spoke very softly.

'My daughter is an addict.'

'Cocaine?'

'Heroin. They keep her supplied; they used the threat of her having an overdose by mistake to get me to play ball.'

'By mistake?'

'Yes.'

'In other words, they would administer an overdose if you refused to go along with them.'

'Yes. I don't get any money, the delivery chaps aren't ours which is why we don't show them on the screen. They work for the Arifs, they just use our wi-fi system.'

Palmer noticed Gheeta and Knight were in reception.

'That's more like it, Mr Court. The more help you give me, the more help I'll give you. Now, which one of your dispatchers is the Arifs' man?'

'What?'

'Which one of the dispatchers is working for the Arifs? One of them is because the Arifs, or their people at the takeaway won't be ringing in like a normal punter, or the job might go to one of your real delivery boys if it went through the Deliver-Eat system. No, they ring a special number which probably comes direct to one of those dispatchers on the other side of this room who is an Arif employee.'

Hhe paused for a moment.

'Don't look now, but I think it is the chap on the far-right console; he hasn't stopped watching us since we came over here. Would I be right?'

Court nodded.

'Yes.'

Palmer waved through the glass partitions to Gheeta and Knight to come in and waited as they walked through the desks; all heads were turned to them now as Gheeta was in uniform. They came into the despatch room and joined Palmer, who spoke quietly to them.

'Don't look now, but the dispatcher on the far right is one of the Arif's people. Arrest him for being involved in drug dealing, but do it fast; I don't want him having time to send an alert out by phone or text. Cuff him and take him to the car. Be careful, in case he has a knife.'

'I'll lead,' said Knight to Gheeta.

He sauntered slowly over to the dispatchers with Singh behind him. He acted as though he was interested in the wall screen, pointing at it until he was within a few feet from the end dispatcher. Suddenly Knight took two fast steps to behind the man and pulled his chair backwards at such a speed that he fell backwards onto the floor, where Knight twisted him onto his face, pulled both arms behind him and had the cuffs on in seconds. Gheeta stepped forward and pulled the phone jack plug from the console socket, unplugged the laptop that the dispatcher had been using and closed it. Knight pulled the man to his feet and slammed him face first against the wall; Singh went across and told him why he was being arrested and read him his rights. Knight patted him down, emptied his pockets and found a rather nasty six-inch blade knife velcro-strapped to his right ankle. He pulled it off and showed it to the man.

'Tut, tut, tut, I don't think this is for cutting your sandwiches, is it? Mandatory five years now for possession of a knife – unless you've got previous, which you probably have, then it's up to the judge what he adds on.'

He roughly pushed the man out through the call centre to the squad car, followed by Singh carrying the laptop.

Palmer went to the glass double door and addressed the startled staff.

'Excitement over for today – carry on as normal please, nothing to worry about.'

Of course the hubbub was never going to die down straight away after that little episode. He turned back to Court.

'Calm them down, Mr Court. Phones are ringing, people want their takeaways.'

Court nodded and spoke loudly to his staff.

'It's all right everybody, nothing to do with us. Carry on please, all finished now – back to business.'

The place calmed down.

'Now I suggest you ring your solicitor, Mr Court. Tell him to meet us at the Yard. Do you have a coat?

'What? Why have I got to go with you? You got their man.'

'It's a triple murder enquiry, Mr Court. You are involved, so I need a statement.'

'You're kidding, I can't do that. What about my daughter?'

'Where is she, at home?'

'No.'

Court paused and looked painfully at Palmer.

'In a squat.'

Palmer understood the implications of that.

'Okay. What about the wife and any other family members?'

'Divorced. I have two sons who are with her.'

'Where?'

'Scotland, Inverness.'

'Do the Arifs know about them.'

'I don't think so, they never mentioned it.'

'Good. I'll have Social Services meet us at the Yard, and when we have your statement you can take them to wherever your daughter is and they will take her into a secure protective rehabilitation hostel. After that you can collect anything you need from home and then you'll go into a safe house until this is over. Understand?'

'What about the business?'

'You must have an assistant who can manage it, what happens when you're on holiday or ill'?

'Yes, yes I can get it covered.'

He indicated a young chap leaning over a telephonist in the call centre.

'John can manage it, he's Assistant Manager.'

'Right, do that now then. Tell him you've got a family problem come up and could be away for a few days.'

****

CHAPTER 11

It all went surprisingly well. Court gave a long statement. He couldn't identify the Arifs from their mugshots, which wasn't surprising as they always stayed 'off camera' and had others do their business for them, so Palmer couldn't get an arrest warrant on them. Their dispatcher had a solicitor at the Yard almost before he was after his *one entitled phone call*, and a stream of '*no comment*' answers was the outcome of his interview with DS Knight, but that was to be expected. Court's daughter Helen was pulled from the squat by Social Services and the local police using a quickly signed judges warrant for 'protection of an underage person in danger' order, and Court was taken to a safe house in Ruislip.

****

It was getting towards late afternoon, and Palmer was thinking of calling it a day after he had read through the transcript from Court's interview, when the call from AC Bateman's office came in summoning him upstairs.

He walked across to the Team Room where Singh and Knight were doing their daily report sheets as Claire updated the progress chart. It had taken the threat of disciplinary action in an official note from the records office to get Palmer finally to complete the Daily Report sheets that Bateman insisted on having and get them up to the fifth floor for his perusal.

'You three get off home when you've done those damn reports – good day today. Tomorrow I think we will get back on track to find the killer, and from what you said Knight, I think we ought to take a closer look at this Wellbeck character.'

He gave them a nod, which was the nearest Palmer ever came to a compliment.

He took the stairs to the fifth floor, gave a hardly audible tap on Bateman's door and went in. Bateman was watering his pot plants on the windowsill with a small watering can and jumped when Palmer entered unexpectedly, causing the can to water his shoes.

'You are supposed to wait for me to say 'come in' when you knock Palmer, not just barge in. I might have been having a meeting, or be with somebody else.'

'Sorry sir', Palmer lied. 'I was told you wanted to see me?'

Bateman rubbed his shoes with a cloth.

'Sit down, Palmer.'

Palmer sat in the 'guest' chair in front of Bateman's large desk, and Bateman sat in his 'power' chair behind it. It was common knowledge that the 'guest' chair in Bateman's office was shorter-legged than Bateman's own chair, so that he adopted the 'power' position of having his guests having to raise their eyes to meet his – a well-known tactic amongst recruitment and personnel people. It was also a well-known Bateman tactic amongst his senior officers, who usually declined the offer to 'sit down' and stood by the desk, making Bateman the one to have to raise his eyeline. Today Palmer couldn't be bothered.

'This delivery boy serial murder case,' Bateman began. 'I see you have seconded one of Organised Crime's officers?'

He raised his eyebrows as a question mark.

'I could do with a couple more, too.'

This was not the answer Bateman wanted.

'I think you are deliberately missing the point, Palmer. Any transfer of officers between departments has to be authorised.'

'DCS Long authorised it, sir.'

'By *me*, Palmer, authorised by me and this office, and by formal request using the correct paperwork.'

'It was rather urgent. Three murders already, and Forensics led us to believe them to be drug-related so it seemed obvious to get an experienced narco officer on board.'

'Narco?'

'Narcotics. I really could do with some extra bodies too, sir. We seem to have stumbled into a drug war – need some surveillance officers, five or six should do it. I'll do the paperwork tomorrow.'

Palmer made to stand and leave.

'Sit down, Palmer.'

'Is there something else, sir?'

Bateman knew he was being tied in knots. He hated Palmer. Palmer was all that Bateman didn't like about the police: old school detectives with great arrest and case clear-up records that skipped and ignored, or tried to ignore, all the reporting and other paperwork that he thought so important. He was right of course; if you went to trial with any piece of required paperwork missing, the eagle-eyed criminal defence lawyers of today would seize on it as a 'non disclosure' item and get an acquittal. But how he got that into the mindset of the likes of Palmer's old school *'chase 'em, nick 'em and bang 'em up'* method of policing was proving difficult, which is why he had offered the likes of Palmer and Long early retirement packages with enhanced benefits, in the hope they would accept them and leave. All had been rejected. He decided it wasn't worth the effort.

'No, nothing else Palmer.'

He knew that once this case got out to the press and media, being a serial murder it would make headlines, so the last thing he wanted was for the case officer to complain he hadn't enough officers. Palmer wouldn't do that publicly of course, but over the years in the force he had made many friends in the media, and a quiet private word here and there would instigate a story about *'cut-backs affecting the progress of the case'* from an *'unnamed source'*.

'Get the paperwork to me and I'll see you have the resources you need.'

Bateman waved a dismissive hand.

'Thank you, sir.'

Palmer was smiling inside. He took the stairs down to his floor two at a time as a self-congratulatory skip in winning that round with Bateman. When his sciatic pain stabbed his right thigh halfway down, he reverted to painful single steps and cursed his exuberance.

****

When the Serial Murder Squad needed extra people, Palmer had a list of well-trusted and seasoned detectives that he had worked with over the years who would be very willing to sacrifice their day off to come in and help him out. Plus, of course, they got paid overtime rate. So it was no surprise to Gheeta that the first four she phoned on his behalf were only too pleased to come in; whether their wives or girlfriends were equally as pleased, we will never know.

The next morning they sat in the Team Room. Gheeta and Knight brought them up to speed as Palmer took a quick trip down to OC and had DCS Peter Long go through the file on Sammy Wellbeck. It was quite a thick file. Long made a copy and Palmer scurried back up to his department.

'Aha! Familiar faces.'

He beamed at his new foursome.

'Well, Messrs Harvard, Trent, Patel and Russell, welcome back lads. Good to have you with us again.'

All murmured their happiness at being there, and it was an honest happiness. Detectives and uniformed officers genuinely liked to work with Palmer and any of the other, now dwindling, old school officers. They knew that Palmer had come through the ranks; he'd walked the nasty beats, he'd roughed it with the villains who wouldn't be taken quietly, and he'd done it before tasers and silly stop-and-search laws and no-win-no-fee lawyers had taken every lying utterance from a villain complaining that he had been assaulted at the police station as gospel truth; then they wasted days of police time in court trying to manufacture a false case to make a claim and keep half of it in fees. Since he took over the Serial Murder Squad it had a one hundred-percent case-solved record which went down well with his detectives and with his political masters, although not so well with AC Bateman and the fifth floor, who found it a barrier to getting rid of him through enforced retirement.

'Okay then,' Palmer continued. 'I think we have disrupted the Arifs' delivery system, but the question now is do we go after them or do we go after the Wellbecks? I think we go for the Wellbecks because we think they are responsible for the killings. Knight here has experience in the OC drugs department, so his input is paramount. I have just had a briefing with DCS Long on the Wellbecks, and I get the impression they are a very nasty bunch. DS Knight?'

He handed the floor over to Knight.

'Very nasty,' Knight said, taking the reins. 'Sammy Wellbeck and his wife Chrissie have ruled the London Central drug scene for about fifteen years. They are a very business-like firm; their base is a scrapyard in Hackney which has a Fort Knox type security system: CCTVs everywhere, a solid tall wall with razor wire on top, and two trusted lieutenants who have been with them since the early days. We've raided them twice when we've had good intel that drugs were on the premises and both times they've come up clean. Forensic swabs showed that cocaine had been there but we couldn't even find a speck of it. They knew we were coming.'

'You've got a leak?' Palmer said.

'We must have. Our information was good, but Organised Crime is a big department and to do a raid with Firearms people involved as well means a lot of officers are in the loop.'

'How did the Wellbecks start? Claire asked, scrolling her monitor screen. 'There's absolutely nothing on file.'

'There won't be – as I said before they are a very clever pair, always out of the picture; experts in delegating others to arrange and carry out their work. They had the usual early career, started by offering protection to clubs and pubs – if the club or pub refused, he sent a few idiots in and they would start a fight and do as much damage as they could. Next day in went Sammy or one of his men again, and this time the owner was more open to a deal on protection. He'd get a couple of doormen from Sammy, and Sammy would install a row of fruit machines and take the money, plus he'd supply a lot of the booze from stolen lorries at cheap prices for cash; he ended up with most of the licensed premises in his pocket. Then he went into the second-hand car and scrap metal business, bought the yard and bribed his way into most of the car insurance companies to take their write-offs at a standard price; makes a fortune from the parts his mechanics salvage and sells on the rest as scrap to the steel companies. That's the legal bit. The illegal bit is the cocaine. We reckon he is amongst the top ten narco importers in the UK. He gets his supply from Peru, and he pays on receipt, as do most of the major importers...'

'On receipt?' Palmer interrupted. 'Nothing upfront?'

'No,' Knight carried on. 'There is so much of the stuff available from South America that the cartels reckon they can lose a third to customs searches and the DEA and not worry. The profit is huge. Most of it comes in by private Cessna – so-called *business flights* landing at small provincial airports in the dead of night, or fishing boats taking it onboard in the middle of the ocean beyond the Border Control boats and landing it with their fish.'

'I thought a lot of it came with so-called mules in air travel baggage? Or swallowed?' Gheeta said.

'No, what comes in that way is tiny. Some of the smaller gangs still do that, but not the big boys.'

'Tiny?'

Knight laughed.

'Well, not tiny to us I suppose. Somebody swallowing a quarter of a kilo of charlie has about ten thousand pounds street value inside them, and some swallow a lot more than that.'

'Or stick it up their arse,' commented one of the new detectives.

'Oi!' Palmer said, waving a finger. 'Ladies present.'

'Sorry.'

Gheeta smiled and turned to Claire.

'We've heard a lot worse than that in this room, haven't we Claire?'

Claire nodded.

'We have indeed, a lot worse.'

They both looked at Palmer.

'Carry on Knight,' he said quickly.

'Okay, so you will now have got the impression that Wellbeck is not to be underrated. We reckon he moves about thirty kilos onto the streets a month.'

'That's a lot of money.'

Palmer seemed impressed, and in fact he was. He had often been impressed – now and in the past – by the way criminals organised themselves and their very business-like ways. He had once suggested, albeit flippantly, at a meeting of DCS's that perhaps some of the government ministries could take a leaf out of the criminal business book. It went down well with the other DCS's, but not so well with the ACs or Home Office staff that were present.

'Yes, a lot of money – and the Wellbecks aren't going to let anybody else snaffle any of it. They hit hard and leave no trace.'

'Right then,' said Palmer. 'We need to find that red Transit and tie it to Wellbeck. We know it has fake number plates, but we have tyre prints from the Jack Bernard crime scene – find those and we find the killer. Be nice to have a look inside that scrapyard. Do the Wellbecks know you, Knight?'

'No, we always wear balaclavas on raids.'

'Good. Right then.'

He pointed to his new recruits.

'Split into pairs: Harvard and Trent, you two do surveillance on the Arifs' takeaway, see who's going in and out, get some pictures; Patel and Russell, same at the scrap yard. Send the pics back using laptops Sergeant Singh will give you, then Claire can run them through our face recognition programmes. You never know, we might pick up a mug shot that rings bells.'

He turned to Gheeta and Knight.

'You two need to purchase something at the car parts counter at the scrapyard when it's open, and keep your eyes peeled for a red Transit.'

'I can film it, sir,' Gheeta said with a smile. 'We will be in civvies so I can use a lens broach and data recorder.'

Palmer looked at the others.

'She never ceases to amaze.'

****

CHAPTER 12

Saturday was a nice day and the late autumn sun was out, which had a lifting effect if you were stuck in a car all day watching a surveillance target. DS Singh met DS Knight at a public car park a few hundred yards away from the scrapyard.

'Nice car,' said Knight, coveting Gheeta's hybrid Range Rover. 'Serial Murder Squad obviously pays more than Organised Crime.'

He pointed to his five-year-old Fiesta. Gheeta laughed.

'I have a generous daddy.'

This was partly true. Gheeta was a director in the family IT and surveillance components company, built up by her father and now run by her two brothers; the car was part of the remuneration package she got annually as a 'consultant'. The other part was the fifth floor Barbican apartment overlooking the Thames. Palmer was aware of this supplementary income and wasn't bothered one bit – except on the days that he parked his seven-year-old Honda CRV next to the Range Rover in the Met car park and quickly suppressed a twang of jealousy.

'Hang on a minute while I fix this.'

Gheeta was wearing a three-quarter length coat with large shiny buttons. The top button hid a camera with a lead inside the coat to a digital chip battery and transmitter in an inside pocket, that sent the signal onto the Team Room where Claire and Palmer waited. She had contact with them via an earpiece hidden beneath a large bobble hat that she had pulled down over her ears, and a small microphone engulfed in her scarf. She finished and smiled at Knight.

'Bit like a human edition of a dashcam, eh?'

She spoke into the mic.

'Singh to Team Room, can you hear me?'

Claire came back.

'Loud and clear, and we also have a picture.'

Gheeta nodded to Knight.

'All ready to go.'

****

The scrapyard was very busy, with customers queuing to purchase car parts and staff scurrying around inside the warehouse pulling them off the shelves. Beyond the sectioned-off public part three swivel cranes were working, lifting the remnants of stripped vehicles into crushers and the crushed cubes that came out into large skips. Rows of stripped cars, vans and lorries awaited their fate.

'Impressive, eh?' Knight said to Gheeta.

'I didn't realise it was so big. You can't tell from outside.'

She walked slowly, trying to get as much footage as she could down the line to Claire.

'Pity we can't get around the back.'

She nodded towards the office block which blocked the view of half the yard.

'You getting this, Claire?'

'We are, good clear picture too.'

They joined the queue in the warehouse for parts and shuffled forward to the counter in line. Knight asked for a Fiesta windscreen wiper motor.

'Mine's on the blink.'

The salesman went off and a few minutes later came back with one.

'How's that then?' he said with a smile. 'Fully guaranteed to work and been overhauled and tested. Ten quid.'

Seeing that it would have been over sixty pounds from Ford, Knight was very pleased and paid. They left the warehouse and walked slowly round the public yard.

'No red Transit in view, but we can't see behind the office block. Could be there.'

As they walked slowly towards the gate, the door to the office block opened and Wellbeck came out with two men. Gheeta stopped and turned, pointing the button camera their way.

'We have personnel coming out of the office.'

Knight knelt and pretended to tie a shoe lace as Gheeta kept the camera on the three men. Knight identified one with surprise.

'Jesus! That answers a few questions!'

'What does?'

Knight turned his face away from the trio.

'Wellbeck's the smaller one in the smart suit. The one talking to him is DI Kirby, my senior officer. Christ! No wonder we never found anything here on the two raids we did – Kirby's warning him, the bastard. Make sure you get pictures of them together. I don't know the other chap.'

'I do.'

Palmer's voice came on Gheeta's earpiece.

'Keep on him as long as you can. His name is Ronny Robards, I thought he was dead. Must be in his eighties by now.'

'Why would he be here, sir? Is he in the scrap business?'

'Sort of,' Palmer said, sounding worried. 'He blows things up.'

****

Back at the Team Room after Gheeta and Knight got back, Claire replayed the camera film. Palmer had it stopped at Ronny Robards and got her to enlarge it.

'Yes, that's him.'

Palmer was sure.

'Got quite a long charge sheet, hasn't he?'

Gheeta had pulled it up on her monitor.

'But nothing for fifteen years?'

'I think he'd had enough after his last spell inside. Told me he was going to retire and enjoy his garden. He grew prize chrysanthemums – I remember we arrested him one time just after he'd collected a gold medal at some flower show.'

'You said '*he blows things up*'. What did you mean?'

'Just that. Ronny was the top man if you wanted a safe blown open or a demolition job. His heyday was in the eighties when the banks installed time reactive safes and vault doors; you couldn't pick the locks or force them open anymore, so the only way was *bang*! Then when the ATMs came in he was in great demand to blow the front off them, so the villains could reach in and take the money. Then they got more secure and Ronny was out of work, except when a security van was robbed and he would blow the back doors off for a fee. He was good, he always knew how much Semtex or gelignite to use; seldom injured anybody.'

'So what is he doing with Wellbeck?' Gheeta asked.

'Yes, that's the worrying bit,' Palmer said, shaking his head. 'I don't think he just popped in for a cup of tea and a chat about old times, that's for sure. I think we ought to keep a good watch on the Arifs' takeaway.'

He turned to Claire.

'Get a blow up of his face out to Harvard and Trent. If he shows up there, we know the plan is probably to blow it up.'

He walked to the Progress Chart on the wall which Claire had updated with pictures of the Arifs and Wellbeck. Lines of access ran from Wellbeck to the victims, and from the Arifs to Court. Gheeta joined him.

'The Arifs must be pretty confused by now, guv. They've lost their Deliver- Eat scam and they know that Wellbeck has declared war on them. What do you think they'll do?'

'People like that don't give a damn about a few delivery lads being taken out – plenty more with mopeds to fill the gaps. They've probably got a tie-in with a couple of the postcode gangs to do the delivering, so no user is going to go without their little packet of fun.'

He checked his watch.

'Right, that will do for today. I have an important celebration to attend – not important to me, but Mrs P. will not be pleased if I don't make an appearance. We've got the two surveillance teams in place so if anything breaks they can get hold of us.'

'What about Kirby, sir?'

Knight was still angry.

'Let him run,' said Palmer. 'He doesn't know we are after Wellbeck, and if we get Internal Affairs to pull him now Wellbeck will know something is up. Keep it between us for the time being.'

'Okay, I think I'll hang about and pop down with Harvard and Trent,' said Knight. 'Give them a bit of break.'

'Okay, up to you. I want twenty-four-hour surveillance on the takeaway, so send one of them home to get some sleep and he can relieve the other one in the morning. Give Patel and Russell a bell at the scrapyard to do the same.'

Palmer was a little worried.

'If Ronny Robards turns up at the takeaway to order a meal, don't let him get inside the place. Arrest him on suspicion, and don't be too rough – no throwing him on the ground to cuff him. Semtex is pretty unstable.'

He gave Knight a wry smile.

'Long wants you back in one piece.'

Gheeta stood up and slung her laptop into its shoulder bag.

'I think I know a way of getting into the scrapyard and having a look round.'

Palmer waved a stern finger at her.

'No, no way are you to go near that yard. Absolutely not.'

Gheeta smiled.

'I'm touched by your concern guv, but I won't be scaling the wall or anything like that. I won't even be going near it. But a drone could get right inside.'

Palmer thought for a few moments. He knew from past experience that Singh's use of technology had, on more than one occasion, solved a case. He looked her in the eye.

'Okay, I'll leave that one to you. Now, I must go – see you all in the morning. I know its Sunday, but time and crime never stop. Goodnight, all.'

****

CHAPTER 13

Palmer fancied a pint. He wasn't a canapés and wine person, and after all he wasn't driving as he had got a cab to bring him to Benji's party from home so he could indulge a bit. Nodding and making polite conversation as Mrs P. guided him around the large function room wasn't his scene at all, but he suffered the small talk to keep her happy. Benji had been glad to see him – so glad was his welcome that Palmer had to give him a fixed glare to stop getting a peck on the cheek; Palmer's cold fixed glares were legendary, they could freeze the sun. Once the tour of the guests had finished he told Mrs P. he was off to get a pint and made his way to the bar, where Councillor Monty Montague was holding court with some of his junior staff from the council offices. Councillor Monty Montague was the last person Palmer wanted to see, the epitome of everything he disliked in a person.

Being an abrasive-tongued senior and longstanding member of the council gave Montague the idea that what he said mattered; it didn't of course, but council staff do like to keep in with their paymasters, so whatever he said they were bound to mutter agreement with.

When Benji was elected to the council on an independent ticket at the last local elections, Montague found he had an opposition member who would question his pronouncements if the facts were not correct; and an awful lot of councillor Montague's pronouncements were not factually correct. Battle lines had been drawn.

Palmer had no time for his sort and had quite openly told him that he would vote for anybody else but Montague when Montague had asked for his support in his quest to become the local Police Commissioner. Palmer couldn't think of anybody worse qualified for the job, except the current Police Commissioner for his area, who – like most PCs – was a failed lawyer who had stood for election as an MP and been beaten, and pulled the old boy network strings to land the cushy PC job.

'Ah, Detective Palmer.'

Montague greeted him with a slimy smile.

'Good evening Councillor Montague,' Palmer replied, without even looking at him.

'Are you enjoying the evening with Councillor Benjamin and his friends?'

'I am, yes.'

He waved a hand to the bar staff chatting at the end of the bar, one of whom came up to serve him.

'Pint of Boddington's, please.'

'I didn't think you were one of *them*, Palmer.'

Montague winked to his listeners.

'One of what, Boddington drinkers?'

'One of Benjamin's lot.'

Montague nodded towards the function room.

'More poofs in there than in a furniture factory.'

He laughed, but didn't seem to notice none of his hangers-on laughed with him. Palmer turned from the bar towards Montague.

'Mr Benjamin is my next-door neighbour Councillor Montague, a great friend to me and my wife and has been for many years. No, I am not *'one of them'* as you so crudely put it – I am, as you know, a Detective Chief Superintendent at Scotland Yard. One more silly peep out of you like the last one and I will arrest you in front of your friends here, put handcuffs on you, and charge you with making sexually and aggressive hate comments in a public place. Then I will call up a car and have you taken away. Understand that, Councillor? Do you?'

Out came the Palmer glare. Councillor Montague suddenly found himself bereft of company as his hangers-on seemed to disappear like mist in the morning sun. He was red-faced. He leant towards Palmer.

'You'll regret that, Palmer.'

Palmer put his face very close to Montague's.

'Your breath smells. Piss off.'

Montague hurriedly pissed off. The barman, having witnessed the exchange, smiled at Palmer.

'Thank you for that, Mr Palmer.'

'For what, son? I didn't do anything.'

'You did, sir. I'm gay and in a civil partnership. You just boosted my faith in the police.'

Palmer raised his glass to the lad and took a gulp.

'Never lose faith, lad. It's a thin blue line, but it will never be broken by the likes of him.'

He went back into the function room carrying his pint, to rejoin Mrs P. with a noticeable bounce in his step and half a smile on his face.

Mrs P. looked at him with knitted eyebrows.

'What have you been up to, Justin Palmer? You look like the cat that got the cream.'

'Nah, more like the cat that got the rat. Can we go home soon, princess? The Arsenal match is on *Match of the Day*.'

****

CHAPTER 14

'It's not very big is it.'

Palmer stated the obvious. It was Sunday morning, and he, Claire and Knight were looking at the drone Gheeta had brought into the Team Room and placed on a table.

'We don't want a big one, do we guv? The bigger it is, the more likely to be seen,' said Gheeta.

Palmer had to agree.

'True. Is this your latest toy?'

'It's state of the art, came into the family business last week. Chinese, of course.'

'Doesn't matter, if it does the job.'

'It *will* do the job, guv. It's silent, got a range of a thousand meters from the controller, has a precision-adjustable micro camera lens slung underneath which transmits pictures continuously back to a recorder chip in the controller in colour. It has four lithium batteries, with a five-hour flying life.'

She picked up what Palmer took to be a controller similar to the Playstation ones his grandchildren had, only this was a little bigger and had a protruding joystick and an eight-plasma inch screen attached.

'And this is the magic box that makes it all happen,' Gheeta continued.

'How much?'

'What, guv?'

'How much would that cost to buy?'

'Seven hundred quid. Shall I order you one?'

Palmer laughed.

'No way, I was just wondering what Finance would say if we damaged it and had to pay up.'

'Don't worry, it's a sample. They sent three.'

Palmer was astounded.

'Three? Over two grand's worth of kit for free? No wonder the Chinese are doing so well. The only sample I ever had for free was an unrequested incontinence pad for old men through the post.'

'Did it fit, guv?'

Palmer quelled the laughter.

'All right, that's enough. Let's get a squad car and put the drone to the test. I take it the pictures can be sent into Claire and recorded? You never know, we might find something useful for evidence.'

'All sorted, I've programmed our wifi password into the transmitter.'

She turned to Claire.

'You'll get the pictures as it happens onto the monitor screen, so when they start coming through click 'share' and open a file to accept them.'

'Okay.'

****

They pulled into the same car park Knight and Gheeta had used the day before. Being Sunday it was empty so they were able to set up the drone and the controller without raising any interest, or any inquisitive noses being poked in by passers-by.

Palmer spoke into the comms handset.

'This is Palmer. Who's on duty at the scrap yard?'

'I am sir, DS Patel. DS Russell was on the night shift and is getting some sleep.'

'Okay, any signs of life?'

'No, all quiet. Can't be totally sure nobody is in there though, as Wellbeck's Range Rover went in earlier and left after about half an hour. But it's got reflective windows so couldn't count them in and count them out.'

'Okay. We are going to send up a small drone to take a look at the parts of the yard that we haven't been able to see from ground level, so don't be surprised if you see it hovering.'

'Shouldn't be able to see it from here, sir – I am about a hundred yards away, parked off the access road. I can see the entrance but not much else.'

'That's fine, I'll come back to you when we are finished. Over and out.'

He nodded to Gheeta.

'Okay, let's go.'

'Right, here we go then. Fasten your seat belts.'

Gheeta clicked a switch and sat in the back seat of the squad car with the door open, manipulating the two joy sticks.

'Why two sticks?'

Palmer was intrigued. Any new technology that could help his squad to do their job was to be embraced, and he liked to keep his non-technical brain in the loop as far as he could.

307

'One for direction – that is forward, backwards or sideways – and the other for up and down.'

'Right.'

Under her control the drone lifted into the sky – above the tall walls that separated the car park from the local houses – and moved silently out of sight towards the Wellbeck's yard. Gheeta stood up and put the controller and screen on the bonnet of the squad car so they could all see. The picture was clear, bright and in colour as the drone flew steadily over houses and empty streets, until Gheeta held it hovering over the Wellbeck's yard at about a hundred feet. She rotated the camera as they looked for signs of life.

'Looks empty,' said Knight.

'Somebody could be inside the office, or in the warehouse.'

Gheeta moved the drone down and focused on the warehouse. The doors were closed. She took it back up and directed it along the yard to the front of the office. That door was closed too. She brought it down to about twenty feet and focused on the office. No sign of life, the window blinds down.

'Get it round the back of the office to the part of the yard we couldn't see from your button camera yesterday,' said Palmer.

The drone moved up and over the tiled roof to the rear of the office, where Gheeta hovered it and used the camera to survey the back area. A row of old scrap lorries were lined up with their cabs against the perimeter wall. She swung the camera round to the back of the office. No windows, just a steel door.

'Pretty basic, nothing unusual there.'

Gheeta took the drone down to about twenty feet and turned it so that the camera pointed at the open backs of the line of lorries, and it travelled along them.

'Bit like an elephants' graveyard,' Palmer observed.

'They're lorries, guv. Elephants have four legs and a trunk – big gray things they are.'

Palmer looked at her with half-closed eyes.

'A figure of speech, sergeant.'

'Whoa!'

Knight leant in to the screen.

'Go back.'

She reversed along the line.

'Stop!'

Knight pointed to the image.

'That old removal lorry with the back-loading slope down, can you get a better picture of the inside?'

Gheeta altered the focus and the dim interior of the vehicle became clearer; and the clearer it became, the more in focus came a red Transit van parked inside.

'Well, there's our hit-and-run van. I'll put money on it,' said Palmer confidently. 'The clever buggers, what a place to hide it.'

'Still circumstantial guv, unless we can get in and get Forensics to go over it and match the paintwork with the mopeds' damage.'

'Mmm, have to figure that out – but the circumstantial is strong enough for Bateman to get a warrant, got to be. Take a look at the rest of the… elephants.'

Gheeta turned the drone's camera to look along the backs of the other lorries.

'Shit!' she exclaimed, as the camera turned and Sammy Wellbeck came into view thirty feet away. He was looking straight at the drone, and so was the sawn-off shotgun he was aiming.

Palmer and Knight held their breath and watched as Gheeta worked the joy sticks

310

manically, zigzagging the drone skywards. They heard two faint blasts of gunshot in the distance. The screen went blank.

'What's happened, is it down?' Palmer asked.

'No, I still have it responding but no picture. Look up in the sky towards the yard and see if we can see it. It's at seventy feet and should be coming this way.'

The radio crackled into action as DS Patel reported.

'Two shotgun blasts from inside the yard. Instructions?'

'Stay put, Patel. Somebody was inside, spotted our drone and took a pop at it. Hopefully we got it away in one piece. It might cause a bit of a panic, so keep looking in case he or they come out looking for it. If they do, give us a heads up.'

'Will do.'

'There it is!'

Knight pointed up at the drone as it came towards them, high over the car park. Gheeta brought it down by the car. The camera had a few small holes in the lens and casing where some of Wellbeck's shot had penetrated it. Palmer picked it up.

311

'That was a lucky escape – if we hadn't seen him when we did he'd have had the whole thing down. Come on, let's get out of here before he comes looking.'

****

Back at the Team Room Claire ran the downloaded file on the big screen. She held it at the picture of the Transit inside the removal lorry.

'That's got to be our murder weapon, hasn't it,' said Palmer. 'Right size, right colour, and why else would they hide it?'

Claire ran the film on to the man with the shotgun.

'Hello Mr Wellbeck,' said Knight. 'I hope you have a firearms certificate for that piece of kit.'

'No he hasn't,' Claire answered. 'I've checked. But Christine Wellbeck has. His application was refused.'

'I'm surprised he even bothered to apply,' added Palmer. 'Most villains don't really want us to know they're tooled up.'

DS Patel came on the radio.

'Patel to base.'

'Go ahead DS Patel,' said Claire. 'The boss is here.'

'The Range Rover is back and gone inside the yard, and so has a Kia with Marty Chaplin driving and Harry O'Keefe with him. Wellbeck was in the yard all the time, he just opened the gates for them.'

Palmer leant forward and spoke into the microphone.

'Okay, when is DS Russell due back?'

'He's back now, sir.'

'Good, just keep watch then. I get the feeling things might be about to happen. Over.'

He stepped back and thought for a moment.

'They're having to make a decision, aren't they? They don't know the drone was ours, so it might well have been the Arifs'; and if it was the Arifs', what was it doing? I think Wellbeck has called in his team and is deciding what move to make. Harvard and Trent, are you both in position near the takeaway?'

'Trent here, sir. Yes, both of us are here. We are about fifty metres up the road from it, parked up. It's all quiet, few customers going in and out and three mopeds parked outside.'

'What about the riders?'

'Inside, somewhere in the back. They're not in the shop part.'

'Okay, probably waiting for enough orders to make a delivery ride. Stay sharp, I've a feeling that things might go off tonight.'

'Will do sir.'

****

CHAPTER 15

Inside the scrap yard office Sammy Wellbeck was pacing the floor. Chaplin and O'Keefe were seated in the comfy seats and Chrissie Wellbeck was behind the counter, silently watching her husband.

'You really think it was the Arifs?' she asked.

'Who else would it be, some kid's toy gone astray? That was a pro job, it made off like a rocket when it saw me. Whoever was controlling it had a camera and was looking for something.'

Chaplin shifted uncomfortably in his seat.

'Could have been the police looking for the van?'

'Police drones are larger, big professional jobs – this one wasn't a police one, too small. I tell you, it was the fucking Arifs looking for a way in to torch the place.'

'So what are we going to do then?' said O'Keefe, spoiling for a fight as usual. 'Why not go and give 'em a hiding at the takeaway?'

Wellbeck nodded.

'That is exactly what we are going to do, Harry. Attack is the best kind of defence.

Those bastards can have another think if they think they are going to walk in here and take our turf.'

'Hang on, Sammy!' said Chrissie, holding up her hands. 'You'll need a few bodies to go and bust up that place, and you'll need to do a proper job or we'll have a war going on and on.'

'So? If they want a war they'll have a war.'

Sammy was not seeing the whole picture. Chrissie was.

'It's not what *they* want Sammy, it's what *we* want. One hit that finishes everything off.'

'I'll get a big team together with a few shooters.'

'No you won't, you'll do nothing of the sort. You'll give Ronny Robards a ring, that's what you'll do. One big hit Sammy, one big hit.'

Marty Chaplin's heart sank. Why is it that when things are going so well and the water's nice and calm, somebody throws in a fucking brick?

The evening started off quietly. Palmer sent out for some sandwiches for the team, while Gheeta went up to the fifth floor. Being the executive floor – the Assistant Commissioners and Home Office Liaison and Administration floor – it had an 'executive' coffee machine that dispensed a brew that vaguely resembled coffee, whereas the machine on Palmer's floor dispensed a brew that totally resembled dishwater.

They sat quietly eating and listening to the Met's radio chatter. Palmer checked his watch: nine o'clock.

'Give it another hour and then I think we'll call it a night if nothing happens. I'm surprised, I would have thought the drone episode would have forced Wellbeck's hand. I've got Mrs P.'s home-made steak and kidney pie waiting at home.'

'I thought you were going vegan?' said Gheeta with raised eyebrows.

'I did. Mrs P. said I was putting on weight, and vegan was the answer. I did it for a week.'

'A week? You're not going to lose anything in a week, guv.'

'I did. A week on a vegan diet and I lost the will to live.'

The radio spoke.

'DS Russell, come in base.'

'Go ahead Russell,' Claire answered.

'The red van has left the yard. O'Keefe is driving and Wellbeck's with him.'

Palmer put down his half-eaten sandwich.

'Here we go.'

He took the mic.

'Palmer here, Russell. Tail it, I think it's probably going to the takeaway. Are Chaplin and Chrissie Wellbeck still inside the yard?

'Yes, they opened and shut the gates for the van.'

'Okay, out.'

He gave the mic back to Claire.

'Keep all the comms open Claire, so everybody can hear everybody and know what's happening.'

He stuck his trilby on his head and put on his coat.

'Come along then, let's go and see what Wellbeck is planning.'

Knight parked the squad car behind Harvard and Trent's. The takeaway was doing good business, with plenty of punters ordering or picking up meals; several sat in the window seats eating from foil trays or paper cones. The mopeds were parked outside. A delivery lad came out, swinging a plastic carrier with what appeared to be small food boxes inside.

Palmer peered forward.

'Whatever is in that bag isn't for eating.'

The delivery lad put the bag in the pillion box and sped off. Palmer spoke into the radio. 'Where are you now, Russell?'

'The van is just turning off the Charing Cross Road to where you are, sir. We are two cars behind it.'

'Okay, if the van parks up do the same and keep your eyes open. Tail it if it doesn't stop.'

The three of them looked towards the Charing Cross Road and saw the red Transit slowly coming down the road.

'There it is, guv.'

Gheeta pointed as the van pulled in fifty yards from the takeaway and parked. Its lights went out.

'What are they up to then?'

'Could be waiting for the next delivery moped to leave and then follow it and take it out?' suggested Knight. 'That's the only way they'd know which ones to hit.'

'Could be,' Palmer agreed.

Harvard came on the radio.

'Harvard here. We think we have eyes on the bloke whose mug shot you emailed, Robards. Is that him coming down towards the van from the main road?'

Palmer, Gheeta and Knight squinted into the gloom at the figure in a long fawn coat approaching. It stopped beside the parked van and spoke through the window to Wellbeck, before continuing to the takeaway. The glare of the shop lights confirmed it was Robards. He went into the takeaway.

'What's he up to?'

Palmer was worried.

'Knight, get in there with him and keep an eye on him – he might try to dump an incendiary under a table or something. If you have to buy something, get a cone of chips. I'm a bit peckish.'

They all watched as Knight left the car and followed Robards inside. At the counter Robards bought a tray of curried chips and Knight bought a cone. Robards sat in the window seat and started eating. Knight sat further back on a tall stool and did the same. Palmer watched carefully.

'Don't eat them all, you greedy bugger.'

'What's Robards up to, guv?' Gheeta asked. She was in uniform so had to stay in the back of the car in the shadows. Palmer had asked her to be in uniform so that anybody approaching them earlier in the car park with the drone could be sent away with some explanation about it being the police testing equipment.

Palmer wasn't sure.

'I think he's sussing the place out. Probably seeing how much explosive to use to do damage but not bring the whole building down.'

Gheeta pointed.

'The van's on the move.'

The van's lights were on again and it pulled out from the kerb, drove slowly to the front of the takeaway and pulled up, blocking Palmer's view.

'Russell, what's happening? We haven't got a clear view now.'

'Nothing sir, it's just seems to be waiting. Hang on… Robards has come out of the takeaway and got in the passenger side. Shall we follow?'

'Yes, stay with them and let us know where they are heading.'

They watched as the van drove away down the road, followed at a distance by Russell and Patel's car.

'Well, what was all that about then?' Palmer asked as Knight returned to the car and slipped inside, handing a half empty cone of chips to Palmer and another to Gheeta with a smile.

'I thought you might be peckish too, Sergeant.'

She took the cone.

'Thank you.'

Palmer was still a bit worried about Robards.

'He didn't do anything suspicious, did he? Didn't bend down to tie a shoe lace and stick a magnetic bomb under the table, nothing like that?'

Knight shrugged.

'Not that I saw. He bought his tray of curried chips, opened the paper and ate half of them. Then the van pulled up outside, so he wrapped the paper back round the rest and dumped it in one of the waste bins.'

'Oh Christ, that's it!'

Palmer dropped his cone and knocking Gheeta's out of her hand was out of the car as fast as his sciatica would allow.

'Come on, the bastard's dumped something in that bin with his meal! Clear that shop, get the people out!'

He turned and shouted at Gheeta.

'Show your uniform and get them out!'

They raced across the road. Harvard and Trent followed from their car, realising something bad was happening.

Palmer and Knight ran into the takeaway, yelling as loudly as they could as they entered.

'Police! Get out! Get away from the building, now!'.

The initial stunned reaction of those inside quickly gave way to a realisation they had to do what they were told, as Gheeta in uniform shouted at them as well and waved them out and away. The staff behind the counter stood transfixed until Palmer shouted: 'Bomb!' and then they took the hint and fled out the back.

Within seconds the place was empty, and Harvard and Trent were ushering bemused people further away up the street. Knight looked at Palmer across the empty floor and then at the three large waste bins.

'I don't know which bin he chucked his stuff into.'

'Too late to search. Get out.'

And they both ran from the building across to the other side of the road and took cover behind a car.

'Get Claire to get the Bomb Squad here.'

Gheeta clicked on her radio.

The blast from inside the takeaway blew out the plate glass front and turned the counter and stools into matchwood which it sprayed through the air across the street and parked vehicles.

As the last scorched bits of the now non-existent takeaway floated down around them, Claire's worried voice came over the radio.

'Base to DS Singh, come in? Gheeta, come in. What's happening?'

'We are okay,' Gheeta answered shakily. 'The takeaway has been blown to pieces, but don't think there are any casualties. I think we got everyone out, but get fire and ambulance asap.'

'Will do.'

They stood up and looked across the road to the blackened hole that was the takeaway. Palmer walked across the road, crunching on glass with every step. Knight and

Gheeta followed, then Harvard and Trent joined them.

'Well, that's one way of sending a message to the Arifs.'

'They won't like this, sir,' said Knight. 'They won't just sit and take it, not the Arifs – they'll come back hard. I hope the Wellbecks know what they are taking on. They've just declared war.'

A cacophony of sirens could be heard approaching. Palmer turned to the team.

'Right. Harvard and Trent, you two seal this area, it's a crime scene – don't let any firemen or uniforms get into it until Forensics get here and have a look. Sergeant Singh, get Claire to put a call out to Reg Frome and ask him and his team to attend, and then call Firearms and get an SCO19 unit to meet us at the scrap yard. I think we'd better get to the scrap yard and get those bastards into custody.'

****

CHAPTER 16

The scrap yard gates were closed, but the yard floodlights were on as Knight pulled the squad car over to the side of the road fifty metres away, behind Patel and Russell who joined them.

'I think we will wait for the SCO19 Firearms Squad before we do anything. I don't think Wellbeck and his lot will come out with their hands up somehow.'

Claire came on the radio.

'Base to Palmer.'

' Go ahead Base,' Gheeta acknowledged.

'Reg Frome has arrived at the bomb scene. London Ambulance say no casualties other than minor cuts from flying glass. The whole place is empty, Mr Frome says it looks like whoever was working there has just abandoned it. He's sealed it as a crime scene, working with the local uniform branch. Do you want Harvard and Trent to join you?'

Gheeta looked at Palmer who shook his head.

'No, they can go off shift unless Frome needs them.'

'Okay, SCO19 unit is on its way. Base out.'

'Vehicle lights coming down the road, sir,' said Knight, looking in the rear view mirror. 'Two vehicles.'

'Good, that will be our Firearms Unit.'

Palmer opened his door and got out. The two vehicles sped by, forcing Palmer to jump out of the way. The first was a flat-bed lorry, followed by a white Mercedes.

'Oh Jesus, now the shit will hit the fan.'

Knight jumped out and joined Palmer, watching as the vehicles neared the gates.

'That white Mercedes can only be the Arifs'. It's their trademark car.'

The flat-bed stopped twenty metres from the gates, did a three-point turn and accelerated in reverse straight into them. The metal buckled and shrieked as the chains snapped and the gates flew open, waving like butterfly wings. The lorry went on into the yard and slewed round across it, forming a barrier; the Mercedes roared in and pulled up behind it sliding on the yard's dirt, it's front ramming into the side of the lorry and wedging underneath it. Shots rang out from the warehouse, where

O'Keefe stood protected behind the long counter and let fly with an automatic rifle. From the blacked-out windows of the office more lead rained down towards the lorry. Behind it, four men jumped from the Mercedes and joined the driver and his mate from the lorry. They took protection behind it and returned fire.

'Where the hell is SCO19?' Palmer shouted above the din to Gheeta.

She pointed up the road where more headlights – this time with a blue flashing one above them – were bearing down on them.

The Tactical Firearms Squad people carrier pulled up beside Palmer and the lead ARV officer got out the passenger door as his team followed quickly from the side door. All were in full riot gear, from their Kevlar helmets to hard boots, and all carried the usual automatic MP5AP carbines. They could hear the gunshots coming from the yard.

'Sergeant Holt sir, lead ARV,' he introduced himself to Palmer.

'DCS Palmer, Serial Murder Squad,' Palmer replied. He waved towards Singh and Knight. 'DS Singh and DS Knight.'

They nodded acknowledgements to Holt. Then Palmer explained the situation to Holt, ending with:

'What would you suggest we do?'

Holt shrugged.

'Well, by the sound of it we could just let it all peter out and then go in and collect the bodies.'

Palmer smiled.

'Trouble is, I need a live one to stand trial for serial murder.'

Holt nodded.

'I *was* joking, sir. I think we'll get to the gates and block any exit for a start; then I'll get a small team to go in and see what we can do. How many are inside?'

'Well,' said Palmer, doing a quick recap in his head. 'Two Wellbecks – including a woman – O'Keefe, Chaplin and Robards on one side; and the three Arif brothers, their driver and the driver and mate from the lorry on the other. Eleven in all. Mind you, I don't know how many are still alive. Been a lot of shooting going on.'

'Okay, I'll leave a protection officer with you and we'll go and take a look.'

'I'm coming in with you.'

'Are you armed, sir?'

'No, I've got a firearms certificate and have kept up my training but I've never felt the need to carry.'

'Too dangerous in there, sir. Best you stay here.'

'No way. Come on, son.'

Palmer made his way towards the gates. Holt looked at Gheeta for support, but Gheeta just shrugged. She knew from past experience that if Palmer wanted to do something, then Palmer did it.

'Just bring him back in one piece.'

Holt nodded.

'I'll try.'

'Are they all still behind the lorry?'

Chrissie Wellbeck peeped out of the corner of the broken window in the office. Wellbeck loosed off a few rounds from his automatic carbine towards the lorry from the other window.

"Yes, got 'em stuck behind it. Harry's pinned 'em from the warehouse and Marty's over by the cranes.'

'Marty's not much use.'

'What do you mean?'

'Take a look.'

Wellbeck crawled across, keeping well out of sight. He edged up alongside Chrissie and looked towards the cranes. Marty

Chaplin was sprawled in front of a swivel crane. He wasn't moving.

'Bastards, the fucking bastards!'

Wellbeck stood and poured a stream of lead towards the lorry. Chrissie pulled him down out of sight as a torrent of lead was returned and zinged around the room above them. Behind the counter, Ronny Robards was wishing he'd stayed retired. It was safer.

'Where's the bleeding police? Never here when you want them.'

'Your bloody fault all this!' Wellbeck shouted back. 'I said to frighten them, not demolish their bloody shop!'

'Well I think it bloody frightened them all right.'

'You senile old git! Right, Chrissie, keep them pinned to the lorry. I'm going out the back and round the scrap heaps to where Marty is. I can get behind them from there and kill the bastards.'

'What about me?'

Robards was worried.

'If he says another word Chrissie, shoot him too. Stupid git.'

Keeping low he edged around the counter and out of the back door, managing to give Robards a kick on the way.

Palmer had Holt in front of him and two SFOs behind. They edged through the small Judas gate in the right-hand swinging gate into the darkness of the yard and along the inside of the perimeter wall to the rear of the warehouse. Not having night goggles, Palmer was at a disadvantage to the others and made sure he kept close.

At the rear of the warehouse they came to a back door. A padlock held a bolt shut.

'Stand back sir, I'll shoot it off,' Holt said

'No, no no!'

Palmer held his arm to stop him and rummaged in his overcoat pocket.

'Hang on…'

He brought out a pair of lock picks on a key ring.

'Give me some light.'

Holt used his helmet light to illuminate the padlock. Palmer started to probe it with the picks.

'Don't teach you this at Hendon do they, Sergeant. We don't want to shoot it off and let everybody know we are here. Softly softly catchy monkey, or something like that.'

There was a faint audible click and the padlock sprung open. Palmer stood to the

332

side as Holt eased the door open and checked inside.

'All clear, sir.'

Palmer slid silently inside. The warehouse was big, with long aisles of four-level racking with used motor parts stocked on them. Looking along the centre aisle they could see the other moonlit end of the warehouse with a counter strung across it. From behind it Harry O'Keefe was bobbing up and down, taking shots at the lorry.

Holt signalled Palmer to be quiet and nodded to his SFOs, who slipped away sideways into the darkness.

****

Harry O'Keefe checked the floor next to him. Two magazines left for his semi-automatic rifle – should be enough. With a bit of luck, the Arifs would realise they were in an open position and get back in the Merc and piss off. He used the whole of the long counter to pop up from, always a different place and each time he loosed of a volley.

He'd seen the blue lights reflected off the low cloud earlier and wondered where the law was. Probably waiting for reinforcements before coming in. So it took him by complete surprise when a thud to the back of his neck sent him forward onto the dirt that was the warehouse floor. His weapon was seized and thrown away from him, his hands pulled behind him roughly and cuffed. A knee in the back held him to the ground as a tie was looped around his ankles and pulled tight.

He was rolled onto his back and stared up into the balaclava of an SFO officer, who held a finger to his lips. Beside him, another SFO knelt with an automatic pointing at Harry's head. Any thoughts of resistance evaporated from Harry O'Keefe's mind. The officer turned and flashed his torch down the warehouse.

****

Holt saw the three flashes from the front of the warehouse.

'All clear, sir. We have control up front. Come on.'

He walked close against the shelving towering above, close enough to be out of any moonlight that might come through the open front if the clouds above parted. They made their way slowly forward to the counter. Before they got to the end of the shelving they

334

reached the SFOs, who had O'Keefe now gagged and tied to the sturdy base of a shelving strut.

'Is he one of your suspects, sir?' asked Holt.

'He's a definite suspect, Sergeant. At least I'll have one live one to put before the judge.'

An increase in the amount of firing in the yard took their attention.

'Somebody is getting impatient,' said Palmer.

****

CHAPTER 17

Sammy Wellbeck had crawled and edged along behind the piles of scrap metal to the shelter of one of his swivel cranes; above him its open grab claw hung silently, like a creature ready to seize its prey. Sammy could see Marty face down on the dirt five metres out in the open, but there was no way he could get to him without being seen. Probably no point; he wasn't moving and the back of his head was a bloody mess from an exit wound. He needed to get a vantage point before the Arifs saw him. Why wasn't Harry shooting from the warehouse? Don't say they got him too.

He peeped over the crane's caterpillar tracks towards the lorry. There was movement; a volley of shots rang out from Chrissie in the office. He could see the top of one of the Merc's doors open; the Arifs were going to do a runner. There was nowhere else for them to go. They couldn't leave the protection of the lorry, it was all open ground around them. Sammy was convinced – they were going to make a dash for it in the Merc.

He edged up onto the crane and reached up to open the cab door. Shots from the lorry pinged on the steel around him, and he felt a sharp stab of pain as one hit his shoulder. He ducked and felt the blood from the wound start to run down inside his jacket sleeve, not much pain as his adrenaline kicked in. There was a screaming of tyres as the Arifs' driver tried to reverse it out from under the lorry, but it was stuck and clouds of smoke from the tyres spinning in the dirt filled the air. The Arifs couldn't see through it to what Sammy was up to, but he knew what he was up to as he hauled himself by one arm into the cab, hit the start button and the diesel engine shook into life.

He took control of the crane levers. The caterpillar tracks rumbled round towards the Merc and the jib extended like an arm straightening at the elbow, swinging the grab claw over the back of the lorry. Sammy hit the button and it banged down onto the Merc, crushing the roof; screams came from inside as he pulled the lever and the claw shut on the Merc. Sammy lifted it, pushing the lorry out of the way and onto its side, diesel spilling from its ruptured tank and joining the petrol gushing from the car's crushed tank. The mixture ignited with a whoosh and thick black smoke set a curtain across the yard, preventing Palmer's team from seeing what was going on behind it.

The Merc was now swinging thirty feet in the air as Sammy reversed the crane and swivelled it round, so the car and its screaming occupants, who had realised what was happening and were desperately kicking at the doors, could do nothing. The crane trundled twenty yards and Sammy swung the jib to the side and released the claw, dropping the car with a loud metallic smash into the giant jaws of the scrap crusher. He stumbled and fell out of the crane's cab, down to the caterpillar tracks and onto the ground. Weak through loss of blood, he hauled himself on his knees to the crusher, and with a last great effort stood on wonky legs and hit the big red start button before collapsing back onto the ground. Above him he watched the thick. hardened steel jaws close slowly onto the car, surrounding it, before reducing it and its human contents to a six-foot cube. The oil sump below the crusher turned a deep red as the Arifs left this world in a coffin not of their choosing.

Sammy also left this world not in a way of his choosing, but he had a satisfied smile on his death mask.

****

Palmer and Holt emerged slowly from the warehouse as Knight came in the gates with another SFO covering him. He called to Palmer.

'Are we clear, sir?'

'I really don't know. That smoke is blocking our view so be very careful,' replied Palmer. 'I think we are clear in the yard, but there might still be somebody in the office. Wellbeck is somewhere up the yard by the crane, and he's armed.'

They joined together and Holt had one of his SFOs take O'Keefe out of the yard and up to their van. They moved slowly to the burning lorry and checked the two Arif men laying in the dirt. Both were dead. They edged their way slowly through the smoke, looking down the yard to the crane whose grab claw was swinging slowly over the crusher.

'Oh my God,' Palmer said slowly, not really believing what he was seeing. 'He's crushed them.'

They moved slowly to the crane and saw Wellbeck slumped against it. Knight checked his pulse.

'He's had it, sir.'

'I don't think the people in the car have done any better.'

Holt had scrambled up onto the crusher's apron and looked down on the carnage inside.

'I think the chaps from the morgue are going to have a job getting the bodies out of this.'

A bullet whistled past Palmer's head and pinged against the steel of the crane.

'What the...'

They all hit the ground as another hit the steel.

'Stay right where you are.'

The shout came from the front of the office, where Chrissie Wellbeck had them covered with an automatic rifle.

'One move and I open fire. There's eighteen left in my magazine.'

'Nobody move,' Palmer ordered in a soft voice, then he shouted back to her. 'You'll only make things worse. You won't get away, there's an armed response unit at the gates. Put the gun down and your hands up.'

The reply was another ping against the crane's steel.

'Don't be a bloody hero, copper. I know how long I'll be looking at so just be sure, I'm not kidding. One move and I spray the lot of you.'

She moved a step back and beckoned towards the office door. Ronny Robards sheepishly stepped out, fear percolating from every pore of his body. He was struggling with a large suitcase. Chrissie Wellbeck positioned herself behind him.

'We are going over to the van. No funny business, or else.'

She said something to Robards who nodded. Putting the suitcase down, he took a small incendiary flare from his overcoat pocket, ripped the top off which lit it like a roman candle, and threw back it into the office. The whoosh from within and the fierce flames that sprang from the broken windows showed that he had doused the place in petrol before leaving. Chrissie Wellbeck didn't intend to leave any evidence of drug dealing behind.

She prodded Robards in the back of the neck with her rifle and they walked slowly towards the red Transit parked alongside the far wall, where O'Keefe had left it when they returned from torching the takeaway. Robards was having trouble carrying the suitcase; it appeared to be too heavy for him. She took it off him whilst keeping the rifle trained on his head from behind.

'How far do you think you'll get, Chrissie?' shouted Palmer. 'We could cut a deal maybe?'

'A deal?'

She stopped and looked towards him.

'Oh yeah? And what kind of a deal would that be?',

Holt spoke to Palmer quietly, trying not to move his lips.

'My men at the gate say they can take her out with a head shot, sir.'

Palmer looked him in the eyes and shook his head slowly.

'No, I want her for trial. If she shoots first then okay, otherwise hold back.'

Holt conveyed the order as Palmer turned his attention back to Chrissie Wellbeck. He had her attention with the offer of a deal, which was what he wanted. He had no real intention of offering one, let alone keeping it, but he needed to keep her attention; because, as well as Holt and Knight, he could see the drone behind her, hovering silently in the smoky night air above the smouldering lorry. DS Singh knelt beside the lorry, working the control panel.

'What could you offer me?' shouted Palmer. 'How about your suppliers for a start?'

Before Chrissie could answer, the drone dived at speed and slammed into the back of her head. She hit the ground already unconscious as the rifle flew from her hand and slithered across the dirt, spinning like a fan. The suitcase dropped with a thud and burst open, scattering its contents of bundled fifty-pound notes onto the ground like tumbling dice. Ronny Robards, visibly shaking now, raised his trembling hands into the air.

Knight was first to the scene, and roughly pushed Robards to the ground face down and cuffed him before checking his pockets for more flares. He found two.

Palmer strolled over and looked down at him.

'Ronny Robards, what a silly old man you are. You must have a liking for prison food.'

Robards's voice trembled.

'I never knew it was gonna be like this. They said they just wanted that takeaway torched.'

Palmer laughed.

'Torched? You blew the bloody place to smithereens, with no warning to the staff or the punters in it at the time. You could be up on a murder charge if my chaps hadn't cleared it. As it is, I'll have you on attempted murder.'

Robards was shocked.

'What?'

'You heard. Take him away.'

Knight lifted Robards to his feet and handed him over to an SFO, who took him stumbling away to the vehicles outside. DS Singh joined them as medics attended to the prostrate figure of Chrissie Wellbeck.

'I meant to hit her in the back, not knock her head off. Will she live?'

'She'll live,' a medic answered. 'Have a hell of a headache though.'

Palmer pointed to the drone's shattered camera lens.

'How did you manage to steer it without the camera working?'

'More by luck than judgement, guv.'

****

CHAPTER 18

In the Team Room the next morning Claire, Gheeta and Knight were bent over a computer screen when Palmer arrived.

'Couldn't you lot sleep? I was out like a light as soon as my head hit the pillow. Then I woke this morning and I remembered all the paperwork that this case will need to close it down and felt like going back to sleep.'

Gheeta stood up straight.

'Not exactly closed yet, guv. Claire's been digging and hit a snag you'll be interested in.'

'Really?'

Palmer moved to the screen, which was showing a black and white wedding photograph. Claire pointed to it.

'The Wellbecks' wedding day – don't they make a lovely pair? I was just trying to get some background info on them. There's not much on file anywhere, so I checked their name against the local Hackney newspapers and came up with this in the local free newspaper thirty years ago. They like to fill the pages with adverts and local people and events – saves the expense of proper journalists. '

'Look a lot younger, don't they?' Palmer commented. 'Nice picture though. I bet they didn't think it would end up like it has.'

Claire pointed to the tagline.

'It's not the picture sir, it's the description at the bottom. It reads: 'The wedding of local businessman Samuel Wellbeck and Christine Court.'

Knight looked at Palmer.

'Ring a bell?'

'Damn right it does.'

Claire flicked onto another screen.

'So I did a bit of digging on the BMD database and came up with Miss Christine Court's family, and lo and behold, she has a brother. Daniel.'

Palmer ran his tongue over his front teeth as though trying to dislodge a reluctant food particle.

'Seems Mr Daniel Court may not be the innocent person that he professes to be then. Claire, give the officers at the safe house he's in a call and tell them not to let him out under any circumstances. I think we need to have a chat with him.'

DS Singh was confused.

'I don't get this, guv. If he's Wellbeck's brother-in-law, what's he doing letting the Arifs use his company to ferry their drugs around in Wellbeck's manor?

'That, Detective Sergeant Singh, is what I want to know, and what we are going to find out.'

****

In the kitchen of the safe house, Daniel Court sat at the kitchen table looking at his sister's wedding picture printed off the computer by Claire. Then he looked at the birth certificates of himself and sister Christine next to it, both showing the same parents. Finally he looked up to encounter Palmer's stern gaze.

'Care to explain?' Palmer said, his cold eyes drilling into Court's.

Court took a deep breath and sat back.

'I'm not in that wedding picture. In fact I wasn't at the wedding, I wasn't invited.'

'Go on.'

'I never liked Sammy Wellbeck from the first day Chrissie brought him home to meet the family, and he never liked me. For some reason she couldn't see the wood for the trees; I could see he was a nasty piece of work, but the gifts and the good lifestyle he offered turned her head. Only when they were married did she realise what she'd let herself in for, but love is blind; and any case, he wasn't going to pack up his car insurance scams. And it just got bigger. And then into the drug scene, first with the E tablets and then marijuana, and finally coke. She had the big house, the top of the range cars, the designer clothes, exotic holidays and money-no-object life style, so she went along with it.'

'How were you involved?'

'I wasn't. I kept a safe distance. I had the delivery business, and then my marriage went wrong. The wife and the boys went to Scotland, and that left me with Helen...'

'Your daughter.'

'Yes. Without her mother around she got closer to Chrissie; Chrissie became a sort of surrogate mother to her. I didn't mind too much, but then she started going on their social nights with them and got sucked into the glitz and the drugs. Once she was hooked I couldn't do anything about it; she became distant and spent most of her time with them. Drug addiction can take many forms, Mr Palmer – with Helen it overwhelmed her to such an extent she couldn't live without three or four hits a day. I tried to have her seek help but she wouldn't.

She became violent and destructive, and then Wellbeck showed his true colours and kicked her out. She would come round to me sometimes when she needed money, but mostly she lived in squats, begging on the streets.'

'That couldn't have been easy for you to bear, being her father.'

The underlying thought in Palmer's mind was what a weak man Court was not to have done something.

'No, it was far from easy. I hated the Wellbecks, and the hate bore into my every pore. Then I got a visit.'

Palmer was incredulous.

'A religious vision?'

'No, far from it. I got a visit from Mehmed Arif. He knew, he knew everything. He said he could put it right.'

'How would he do that?'

'He was quite open with me, Mr Palmer. He said he had daughters, and if anybody did to them what Wellbeck had done to Helen he'd have them killed.'

'He offered to kill Sammy Wellbeck?'

'No, he had a better offer than that. He would look after Helen's drug supply, make sure she got enough but no more – basically keep her stabilised until I could get her some help.'

'In exchange for what?'

'I told you he was open with me. He said he wanted to get rid of the Wellbecks from the area and take over the drug business, but he needed a supply chain to get the stuff to his dealers, and one that was not going to draw attention as he built his network. My delivery lads would be just the job.'

'So you took the deal, shook hands with the Devil?'

'Of course I did. Helen would be basically back in my control and Wellbeck hit hard where it hurts, in his pocket. Of course I took the deal. Mehmed put his own controller in and I took care to give the delivery to just a few of my better lads. They knew what was involved, but money talks.'

'The Arifs played you, didn't they? They knew that hurting Wellbeck was the button to press in your head.'

'I suppose so. What happens now?'

'Depends on the CPS. They'll probably charge Chrissie with dealing, take the Wellbeck property under the Proceeds of Crime Act, and she will go down for a long time. So will Marty.'

'And me?'

'You need a good lawyer. I would think you've got a 'mitigating circumstances' plea; uou could do time, or you might get a suspended sentence.'

'Will you put in a good word?'

Palmer looked him straight in the eye.

'No. You could have saved me a lot of time and possibly prevented all the killing if you'd fronted up at the beginning. You didn't, you lied. I don't like liars.'

****

CHAPTER 19

Commander Peter Long sat at his desk, looking at the photos of DI Kirby at the scrap yard that Palmer had laid out. He blew out his cheeks with a long breath and raised his gaze to Palmer and Knight sitting opposite.

'The bastard.'

'Always one bad apple in the barrel, Peter.'

'I'll get Internal Affairs to arrest him once we put all this together with your statements.'

'At least he couldn't tip them off this time.'

Knight was worried.

'He's going to deny it. He'll say he was there trying to build a case against them or some such excuse.'

Long shook his head.

'We haven't got any case on file against the Wellbecks, nothing ongoing, so he hasn't a chance with that excuse; and I bet there's no reference to his visit or a visit report on his computer or filed anywhere. He's toast.'

Palmer rose and Knight did likewise.

'Okay, leave it with you. I've a pile of paperwork to get through or Bateman will be whining.'

Long sat back in his chair.

'And where do you think you are going, DS Knight? You still belong to this department, you know.'

Knight was embarrassed.

'Yes sir, I realise that – and I will be back as soon as I've done my reports.'

Palmer turned at the door, a mischievous smile on his lips.

'I was thinking of keeping him actually, Peter. I could do with another DS.'

Long gave Palmer a slanted look with raised eyebrows.

'Oh really? Well I'm afraid you'll have to look elsewhere for your DS. I have a sudden need for a DI, and I always promote from within.'

They both turned to Knight and smiled as his embarrassment turned into happiness.

****

CHAPTER 20

'Sounds more like the wild-west to me than Hackney,' said Mrs P. as she put Daisy the dog's food bowl down on the kitchen floor. Daisy knew just how to play Palmer; she solicited treats and scraps from his plate when Mrs P. wasn't watching that were forbidden when she was. It's funny how dogs favour one person in a house; it's usually the one they can get away breaking the rules with, and Daisy had Palmer firmly in that position.

This evening Palmer was enjoying a home-made steak and kidney pie with chips and mushy peas. Mrs P. straightened up as Daisy got to work on her food.

'You want to remember Justin Palmer, you're no spring chicken now. Bullets don't respect age.'

'We had the Firearms boys with us. Anyway, I didn't get shot – none of my team did. Bateman wants to see me in the morning.'

'Sounds ominous. Why would he want to see you?'

'Might be putting me up for a medal. We just brought down two of the biggest drug firms in London.'

Mrs P. stopped and gave him a sideways look of pity.

'Bateman will never in a million years give you credit for anything, you know that. He's probably going to try and force you into retirement with an enhanced pension.'

'No chance, he could double it and I still won't go. He's tried the same tactic on Peter Long, and he won't go either. All Bateman wants is a row of dickheads with degrees who say 'yes sir' to every stupid idea he has.'

Daisy had finished her bowl and wandered under the table, nudging Palmer's leg. He surreptitiously slid a chip down to her. Mrs P. glared at him.

'Stop feeding that dog from the table. She's had her food. She's half a kilo over weight as it is.'

'I wish I was only half a kilo over weight,' said Palmer, shovelling in another forkful of pie.

'Oh, that reminds me.'

Mrs P. wiped her hands on the oven cloth and left the room. Palmer took the opportunity to pass down two more chips to Daisy before she returned, holding a book.

'Benji brought this round for you.'

Palmer looked at the cover.

'*The Vegetarian Good Food Diet.*'

'He said he noticed how you tucked into the plates of party food at his birthday party. All vegetarian, and he remembered I'd told him you needed to lose weight. Isn't that a nice gesture?

'I was blooming hungry, I hadn't had anything to eat and came straight from work. I would have killed for a sausage roll.'

'And he said to say thank you, I don't know what for but I did notice the barman pointing you out to him during the evening. What had you been up to?'

'Nothing.'

He quickly changed the subject and pointed at the book.

'I hope you're not going to be dishing up veggie dishes all the time.'

'Wouldn't hurt to cut down on the meat we eat. Cows are the biggest source of methane gas.'

'I think Linda McCartney's Veggie Burgers run them a close second. When we had them I couldn't stop far-'

Mrs P. silenced him with a stern finger.

'Thank you, we don't wish to know about that.'

'I thought I was going to take off and go into orbit at one point. No wonder they called their band Wings.'

****

Gheeta sat at her work desk and took a last look down at the Thames rolling by five floors below her Barbican apartment before clicking on her PC and bringing up the family intranet connection. She had set this up so the far-flung members of her family could see and talk in private. It was, of course, encrypted for absolute privacy, and clearer than Skype which was a magnet for hackers.

She checked the thumbnails in the corner of the screen. Her mother was on, and so was Aunt Raani and fourteen-year-old cousin Bavinda in New York. Oh well, better say hello.

She logged in. They all greeted each other.

'We have missed you Gheeta,' said Aunt Raani. 'Have you been working too hard?'

'Always working hard Aunt Raani, time and crime waits for no man. Are you all well?'

'Yes we are, thank you.'

'Which serial killer are you chasing now, Gheeta?' Bavinda asked excitedly. She had long expressed a wish to be a detective in the US SWAT team, much to Aunt Raani's horror.

'Oh, we've caught them now. Just got to write up the reports for the prosecutor.'

'Them?' Bavinda said, sounding impressed. 'How many? Was it a gang? Was it the Mafia?'

'Now, now,' scolded Aunt Raani. 'This is not our business.'

She had no wish for her daughter to do anything other than eventually marry a suitable – that meant rich – young Asian and have a family.

Gheeta laughed.

'It's okay, Auntie. No it wasn't the mafia, Bavinda. Just a rather nasty little group of drug dealers.'

Bavinda nodded.

'Narcos, eh?'

'Where do you learn such words!'

Aunt Raani was not pleased. Gheeta's mother laughed.

'My dear sister, do you not watch television? '

Raani was shocked.

'Not those type of programmes.'

'I do,' said Bavinda. 'Escobar and the Cartels, brilliant on Netflix.'

'When do you watch such programmes, Bavinda?' Aunt Raani asked sternly.

'On catch-up in my room when you are watching those boring food programmes.'

'You should be watching those food programmes yourself,' said Aunt Raani. 'Your father's restaurant is the best in New York, and one day we hope you might be part of it.'

Bavinda grimaced.

'I help at weekends.'

Aunt Raani turned her attention to one of her favourite subjects.

'You must come over next time you have a holiday, Gheeta. Your uncle's restaurant attracts the very best families in New York – many with suitable unmarried sons. I can introduce you.'

This preoccupation with getting Gheeta married off to a 'suitable' family was an enduring topic of Aunt Raani's conversation each time they talked. It seemed to be her quest in life. She herself was an arranged marriage bride, although that was thirty years ago when it was deemed natural. Gheeta's mother was not, and so she and Gheeta's father had no wish to push their daughter into such a partnership; for that was all they were, certainly not marriages. Wisely, Gheeta's mother kept quiet on the subject when her sister started off.

'There's some of the very worst families that come to dad's restaurant as well,' said Bavinda, putting the boot in.

'What!'

Aunt Raani was shocked.

'I hear them talking when I'm serving them at weekends. What about that Deputy Mayor, the one with all the gold chain round his neck? He's always eating with people who he says he will 'see all right'. What he means is he will put council contracts their way. Probably gets a backhander.'

'Bavinda! You must never mention this to anybody else! Nobody!'

Aunt Raani looked as though she might have a heart attack.

'What about the Hussain brothers then?'

'What about them? They are very respected car dealers with luxury car franchises. We have one of their BMWs on lease.'

'So why do they share out wads of banknotes in their corner cubicle every Saturday night?'

Gheeta's mother calmed the situation.

'I think you should watch and keep quiet Bavinda, don't you Gheeta?'

'Yes, you don't know what's going on Bavinda – probably quite legal and above board, so if you said anything you could look very silly. If it's not legal then maybe the FBI are already onto it. I'd steer clear if I was you.'

'I know, I'm not stupid. Mum thinks I am, but I'm not.'

'Anyway, whilst you are on Gheeta,' said her mother. 'It's your dad's birthday in a fortnight and your brothers have booked the Curry Leaf, so you had better make a note.'

Gheeta kept a calm voice.

'Booked where?'

'The Curry Leaf, it has splendid reviews in the local papers and our neighbours have been and recommended it.'

'Where is it?'

'Ilford High Street.'

Gheeta relaxed.

'Okay, remind me nearer the time.'

Aunt Raani seized the opportunity.

'I have several families in London that I know who have suitable sons that could accompany you, Gheeta. I can make some phone calls?'

'Phone calls, Aunt Raani? Am I going to hold auditions? And anyway, who says I haven't already got somebody to go with?'

She could see her mother smile as Aunt Raani's eyes widened.

'You have? Who? What does his family do? What part of India are they from? Does your mother know the family?'

'First I've heard of it,' said Gheeta's mother. 'Gheeta is over 21 you know, Raani. She is allowed to make her own decisions.'

'Thanks, Mum.'

'Yes, yes, yes,' said Aunt Raani, waving her hands. 'But the family must be involved.'

'No way,' Bavida butted in.

'What?'

'No way, Mum. I hope you update your old-fashioned ideas before I'm 21, or we are going to have a lot of rows. I'm 16 in two years and I'll be able to vote, to join the army and to carry a gun. So shouldn't I be able to choose who I go out with too?'

'Yes, providing your father and I agree he is suitable and we know his family.'

'I'll choose him carefully, Mum.'

Aunt Raani nodded.

'Good.'

'He'll be an African-American from a one-parent family, with a record of drug dealing and into rap music. How's that?'

Aunt Raani was speechless. Gheeta thought it was time to end the conversation.

'I have to go.'

'Me too,' said her mother. 'Your father will be home soon for his dinner. Take care, all. Talk next week.'

And she clicked off.

'Cheerio, Aunt Raani. Cheerio, Bavinda, stop upsetting your mother.'

And Gheeta clicked off her camera but kept the audio on. She heard Aunt Raani.

'Your father will hear of this when he gets home.'

'He knows,'replied Bavinda. 'I told him about the crooks in his restaurant, he already knew.'

'And I will take the television from your room.'

'Okay, I'll watch on my phone.'

'Haven't you any homework to do?'

Gheeta clicked off and sat back chuckling. She called over her shoulder.

'You can come out now.'

The kitchen door behind her opened and Raj came in, holding two glasses of wine.

'I hope I'm the one accompanying you to your dad's birthday?'

She took a glass.

'Well, we will have to see, won't we? You may have to do an audition…'

****

CHAPTER 21

Assistant Commissioner Bateman put down the report he was reading as Palmer came into his office. Bateman was not alone. Seated next to him was a rather austere-looking civilian lady, grey hair in a bun and tweeds; she reminded Palmer of Alastair Sim as Miss Fritton, the headmistress who couldn't pay the bills in the original St.Trinians film.

'Sit down, Palmer.'

'I'd rather stand, sir. Bit of sciatica in the thigh.'

It was a blatant lie. All the senior officers knew Bateman used the 'management power' techniques from an array of 'How to Manage People' books on his bookshelf, and one such technique was to have the chair in front of his desk much lower than his own. This gave him the sense of power as he looked down on his officers.

'This is Miss Hardaker from the IOPC.'

He waved a hand at the lady.

'Miss Hardaker has asked to see you as they have had a serious complaint about your behaviour towards a member of the public.'

'Really, sir?'

Palmer's view of the Independent Office for Police Conduct was that is was a lot of busybodies with nothing better to do than chase policemen for doing their jobs. If some nasty drug-pusher got his nose 'accidentally' broken whilst resisting arrest... what a shame.

'Yes, Miss Hardaker has brought to my attention a signed complaint from a Mr Montgomery Montague, who holds public office as a Councillor, that you were obscene and threatening to him in a public place. Ring a bell?'

Palmer smiled.

'Yes sir, I told him to piss off or I would arrest him.'

Miss Hardaker was surprised, if not even startled by Palmer's response. She was used to officers with complaints lodged against them denying the charge; was this officer admitting it? This could result in his suspension.

Bateman knew from that remark that Palmer was on firm ground; no way would he admit to the charge if it had any credence whatever. He may not be Palmer's biggest fan, but after all, Palmer was one of his senior officers; and although there may not be any love lost between them, when an outside force attacks, you close ranks. He sat back.

'Okay Palmer, explain please.'

Palmer did so, in great detail. His final words were the coup de grace.

'It may interest the IOPC to know that at the time of this little episode I was *not* on duty, I was at the pub to attend a private function in a civilian capacity. Any altercation with another person was as a private individual, not a member of the force. Did the IOPC check that?'

Bateman looked at Miss Hardaker.

'Did you?'

Hardaker thought for a moment.

'This was not made clear by the accuser.'

Bateman picked up the report and handed it to her.

'Perhaps you should go back to him and establish the correct facts. You might also make it clear to him that the descriptive language he used, such as *'poof'*, is not acceptable these days, and if DCS Palmer had felt inclined he was well within his rights to issue Montague with a warning about it, or indeed arrest him.'

An embarrassed Miss Hardaker hurriedly left Bateman's office.

'May I go, sir? I have a lot of reports to fill in on the Wellbeck case.'

Bateman ignored the request.

'A word of advice, Palmer. The force and the world it works in is changing rapidly. You know this, otherwise you wouldn't have fought tooth and nail to get DS Singh and her IT knowledge into your unit. But, as it changes so we have to change our ways too, Palmer. We are very much the underdogs today; every move is analysed by some damn unelected quango who have to justify their taxpayer funding, and hauling a very senior officer before a tribunal for overstepping his authority would be a feather in their cap.'

'I didn't over step my authority, sir. I merely pointed out to a man who holds a public service job that remarks of the kind he was making are not acceptable. I am quite aware of the changes in the public perception of the force, sir. We both know that PC no longer means Police Constable, it means Politically Correct. And between you and me, it's a load of lefty tosh.'

Bateman knew he was banging his head against a brick wall.

'Okay Palmer, we will let the subject rest there. Anyway, congratulations on the Wellbeck case. That developed a bit fast, didn't it?'

'Nasty people sir, old school guns and violence. Something Miss Hardaker and her committee wouldn't know anything about. Don't expect they've ever been shot at do you, sir?'

Batemen knew he was not on to a winner.

'All right Palmer, off you go. And let me have the reports as soon as you can.'

****

CHAPTER 22

The Public Prosecutor's Office took two days to assess the best charges to put on the strength of Palmer's reports. Daniel Court received a suspended six-year sentence for aiding and abetting a criminal act, and returned to run Deliver-Eat. They charged Chrissie Wellbeck with conspiring to murder the Arifs, major drug-dealing and money laundering, Harry O'Keefe with attempted murder and drug dealing, and Ronny Robards with attempted murder for the takeaway explosion. All property and bank accounts belonging to the Wellbecks were ceased under the Proceeds of Crime Act, with Wellbeck's scrap yard being put up for sale after gaining outline planning commission for sixty houses.

****

Daniel Court felt a great weight had been lifted off his shoulders and settled back to running his Deliver-Eat business. A week later he got a call from reception that he had a visitor. A tall middle-aged man in a smart blue suit was waiting; could be a prospective new client looking for a reliable delivery service.

Daniel put on his best smile and stretched out his hand.

'Good afternoon. I'm Daniel Court, CEO of Deliver-Eat. How can I help you?'

His hand was taken in a firm handshake.

'Hello Daniel, I know all about you. I think we might be able to do business. My name is Terry Adamson...'

THE END

The Author

Barry Faulkner was born into an extended family of petty criminals in Herne Hill, South London, his father, uncles and elder brothers running with the notorious Richardson crime gang in the 60s-80s, and at this point we must point out that he did not follow in that family tradition although the characters he met and their escapades he witnessed have added a certain authenticity to his books. His mother was a fashion model and had great theatrical aspirations for young Faulkner and pushed him into auditioning for the Morley Academy of Dramatic Art at the Elephant and Castle where he was accepted but only lasted three months before being asked to leave as no visible talent had surfaced. Mind you, during his time at the Academy he was called to audition for the National Youth Theatre by Trevor Nunn – fifty years later he's still waiting for the call back! His early writing career was as a copywriter with the major US advertising agency Erwin Wasey Ruthrauff & Ryan in Paddington, London during which time he got lucky with some light entertainment scripts sent to the BBC and Independent Television and became a script editor and writer on a freelance basis. He worked on most of the LE shows of the 1980-90s and as personal writer to several household names including Tom O'Connor and Bob Monkhouse.

During that period, while living out of a suitcase in UK hotels for a lot of the time, he filled many notebooks with DCS Palmer case plots and in 2017 he finally found time to start putting them in order and into book form. 13 are finished and published so far, with number 14 underway. He hopes you enjoy reading them as much as he enjoys writing them. Faulkner is a popular speaker and often to be found on Crime Panels at Literary Festivals which he embraces and supports wholeheartedly.

He has been 'on screen' as a presenter in television crime programmes including the Channel 5 Narcos UK series, and his Palmer book 'I'm With The Band' has been serialised by BBC Radio.

Faulkner now lives in the glorious Forest of Dean with his wife and three dogs.

Once again, thank you for buying this book.

Stay safe and take care.
****

374

Printed in Great Britain
by Amazon